In the development of this novel the author was inspired in part by actual events connected with the dissolution of the Soviet Union and its aftermath that have been amply reported in the press and literature.

Having made this clarification it is important to emphasize the fact that this is a work of fiction and the situations described, as well as the characters and their actions are totally imaginary.

Having reviewed the manuscript, as required by law, the CIA required the following disclaimer:

"All statements of act, opinion, or analysis expressed are those of the author and do not reflect the official positions or views of the CIA or any other US Government agency. Nothing in the contents should be construed as asserting or implying US Government authentication of information or Agency endorsement of the author's views. This material has been reviewed by the CIA to prevent the disclosure of classified information."

THE DOVE

MRD Enterprises, Inc.
PO BOX 1000
Mount Jackson, VA 22844
mrdenter@shentel.net

Library of Congress Control Number: 2017905637
ISBN 978-0-692-87714-2

Contact author at info@michaelrdavidson.com

Cover by Damonza

Printed and bound in the United States of America.

First printing 2017

Also by Michael R. Davidson

Harry's Rules

Eye for an Eye

Incubus

The Incubus Vendetta

The Inquisitor and the Maiden

Retribution

Krystal

With Kseniya Kirillova

In the Shadow of Mordor

Successor

THE DOVE

It's the 1980's. There are no smart phones and very few mobile phones, certainly not the proliferation of electronic neck benders available to us today, neither was there a Google nor even an Internet as we know it now. Photography was still limited to film rather than electronic pixels.

Espionage had not yet come to rely very heavily on gadgets. Most "advanced electronic" gadgets of the era intended for espionage were beta types and unreliable. They tended to break easily or simply did not work, at all. Agent communications were still in the form of secret writing, short wave radio, one-time pads, and hands-on street work – case officers pumping adrenalin and agents sweating bullets. In other words, what one might term classical tradecraft. It was risky business.

The times were precarious. The Soviet Union, engaged in a debilitating, losing war in Afghanistan, was teetering, but still not vanquished. We still lived in a bi-polar world. The Cold War dominated international relations. The deadly contest between the CIA and the KGB raged on.

And 1985 marked the beginning of problems for the CIA's Moscow Station as its most valuable agent operations were wrapped up one after another by the KGB. The treason of Aldrich Ames would not be uncovered until the 1990's.

Prologue

Moscow – February 1987

Lieutenant Colonel Stepan Timofeyevich Barsikov watched helplessly as Elena Trofimovna sashayed through his office door, giving him an impudent and dismissive twitch of her round derriere. He knew where she was going. She was headed in the direction of the Head of Section, Colonel Yuriy Nikolaevich Lebedev. Stepan could imagine Lebedev's hand snaking up under her dress after they had closed the office door.

Stepan covered his face with both hands as tears started suddenly from his eyes. With as much dignity as he could muster, he rose almost painfully, like an arthritic old man, from his desk and made his way, slightly staggering, out of the office and down the hall towards the restrooms. He needed to splash some cold water on his face. As he passed open doors he could hear the scarcely concealed titters of his fellow workers.

Until just a month ago, Elena had been his. He knew she was the office flirt. Moreover, Stepan had been married for 20 years. Nevertheless, he had fallen head over heels for her, but his infatuation had turned into fixation and fixation had become obsession. His smothering attentions had finally driven her away and into the arms of the office's most notorious lothario.

Stepan's office mates had followed the deteriorating romance with the avidity of afternoon soap opera fans. Lebedev, always one to recognize a good opportunity when he saw one, deftly caught Elena on the rebound, and now Stepan lay awake night after night imagining the depravities to which "his" girl was being subjected by his slick rival.

The ill-concealed mirth of his soulless co-workers spurred his despair towards malice. During his darkest hours Stepan resolved to wreak vengeance on Elena, Lebedev, and the hyenas with which he shared the office. Most important, he would do all he could to destroy the corrupt organization that he served, the Committee for State Security – the KGB.

Stepan was a highly proficient engineer, a graduate of the Bauman Higher Technical School, and a specialist in advanced aircraft design. During his university days his dream was to work at the famed Mikoyan Design Bureau, or perhaps Ilyushin, but his fate had been different. Instead of designing aircraft himself, he had been recruited by the KGB.

In the beginning it had been exciting and rewarding. He was selected for the prestigious PGU, the First Chief Directorate. Already proficient in the French language, he was rewarded with a highly desirable posting to Paris under Trade Mission cover. He had been highly successful, both at recruiting sources within French industry and gleaning restricted technical information that would boost Soviet weapons production. At the end of his tour, he was promoted to the rank of Lieutenant Colonel.

He and his wife, Svetlana, had luxuriated in the glamorous atmosphere of the City of Lights. Stepan in those years was gregarious and convivial, and he was highly intelligent. With attractive Svetlana at his side, it had been easy to cultivate French friends and business contacts. There was a special affinity between Russians and the French that dated from the time of

Catherine the Great.

But things took a turn for the worse in Stepan's next assignment to the Soviet Trade Mission in Montreal. One night, his conviviality led him to one drink too many, and he was involved in an automobile accident resulting in serious injuries to the occupants of the other car. Inevitably, Stepan was recalled to Moscow in disgrace. He would never be given another foreign posting.

That had been ten years ago, and here he sat, still a lieutenant colonel in a dead-end job in Directorate "T" where he evaluated stolen Western aircraft designs and weapons systems. Stepan was no longer a James Bond type. And he was surrounded by the flotsam and jetsam of the KGB.

Directorate "T" was devoted to what in the West would become known as "technology transfer," the illegal acquisition of protected technology for adaptation and incorporation into the Soviet Union's military-industrial complex. This work was accomplished through an incredibly well-organized and extensive network of front companies and espionage operations directed by the Military Industrial Commission, the VPK.

Stepan's personal isolation and deepening sense of despair could not be concealed, and he found himself involuntarily playing the role of office goat, the butt of a steady stream of maliciously ribald jokes. His helplessness in the grip of his own emotions ignited deep within him a waxing desire for revenge that bordered on mental derangement. He was possessed by an inchoate rage that over the days and weeks would take on shape and meaning.

Stepan would have his revenge on them all. When he slept he dreamed of the stricken looks on their faces when their work was destroyed and they became irrelevant. He especially relished the idea that they would know in the end that it had been he who had caused their collective misery.

All he required was the right opportunity.

Chapter 1

Paris, France – April 1987

It was Thursday, which meant that the *plat du jour* at *Le Petit Colombier* was calves' liver, perfectly braised and left a delicate *rosé* in the center. In this case, the dish was *foie de veau en persillade avec pommes de terre,* a Lyonnais version of the dish. A four-year-old Saint Estephe provided a worthy accompaniment.

The restaurant, one of my favorites, was high up on *Rue des Acacias*, a stone's throw from the *Arc de Triomphe.* I frequented the place so often that the staff knew my name. A table on the second floor had become my regular Thursday rendezvous with Nikolay Kozlov. Kozlov was the Novosti representative in Paris and I held First Secretary rank at the American Embassy. Kozlov, of course, was a KGB spook, and I was Chief of Operations for the CIA's Paris station.

In this position, I wasn't really expected to pound the pavement and develop candidates for recruitment, but I still liked to keep my hand in.

According to our file on him Kozlov was thirty-five, several years younger than me, I won't say how many. He carried himself with the grace and elegance of a pre-revolutionary Russian nobleman, and with his careless dishwater blond hair and thin moustache he could have been a 1930's movie idol. I thought there was a slight chance of convincing the Russian that he was working for the wrong side, but truth be told, I enjoyed the verbal sparring with an intelligent adversary/target and the opportunity to brush up on my rusty Russian language skills. Personal interaction with the enemy was the most interesting part of the job.

The waiter cleared the table of the main course and placed generous wedges of *tarte tatin* and small cups of strong coffee before us. Kozlov's elbow was on the table supporting an upraised hand, bent gracefully at the wrist, in which he held a lighted cigarette, a Marlboro. Maybe this was a sign he was vulnerable to Western degeneracy. I rolled an oily Montecristo No. 4 between forefinger and thumb. Maybe the commie across the table thought this meant I was vulnerable to Cuban blandishments. It was only fair.

I decided to wait until I was back in the office to light it and put it back in the breast pocket of my blazer. I didn't think the conversation would last much beyond coffee, and I had decided to walk back to the Embassy, which would delay my afternoon smoke even longer. No one who loves cigars would ever think of smoking one out of doors.

When anyone spoke of the Soviet Union these days the conversation turned inevitably to the Chairman of the Communist Party of the USSR, Mikhail Gorbachev. It was difficult to discern what official Russians abroad really thought of their leader, and Kozlov was no exception.

"I think things are going to change radically in your country, Nikolay," I ventured. "I think they're going to change quite a bit."

Kozlov took a hit from his cigarette and resumed his languid pose. He slit his eyes and squinted across the white tablecloth as he exhaled a cloud of blue smoke. "Never," he said. "Things will never change."

It was hard to tell whether it was conviction or resignation in his voice, so I took another stab at it. "I wouldn't be so sure. Your new guy is shaking things up. Don't you think it's a good thing?"

Now, this was downright provocative, but I was trying to get a reaction. Besides, it was always fun to poke the bear.

Soviets were studiously neutral when asked for their personal opinion on just about anything. You could say the weather was nice, and they'd check with Moscow before answering. But once in a while a fellow got lucky.

Kozlov smiled thinly as he tapped the ash from his cigarette. "What do you think, Harry? Do you think it's a good thing?"

"It looks like it's heading in the right direction."

The Russian took another drag before crushing the cigarette out in the ashtray. "There's your answer, then," he said with a crooked half-smile.

It was impossible to know whether he meant it was a bad thing if I liked it or it was a good thing and I was correct in liking it.

I dropped enough cash on the table to pay the tab, and we walked in single file down the narrow staircase to street level. On the sidewalk we shook hands, and I watched Kozlov turn up *Avenue Carnot* towards the Metro at the *Etoile*, probably on his way to the glitzy modern edifice in the 16th Arrondissement that was the Soviet embassy where he would write a report on our luncheon conversation. Undoubtedly, it would depict Kozlov as besting me through clever use of dialectic materialism. I wondered if the KGB had me listed as a recruitment target or whether they allowed Kozlov to stay in contact just to keep tabs on me. There could be no doubt that they knew who I was. Or maybe he just liked to eat in one-star restaurants on Uncle Sam's tab. I certainly did.

It was a long walk down the length of the *Champs Elysees* to the American Embassy on *Place de la Concorde*, but it was a brilliant spring day and the double rows of elm trees that lined the avenue were sprouting new leaves. They don't call Paris the City of Light for nothing. There is a quality to the air that can't be duplicated. I'd missed my morning run, so the walk would do me good. This made me feel virtuous. I set off down the gentle slope of the most famous avenue in the world blissfully unaware of what awaited me.

I had become inordinately fond of Paris and of the French people. Most Americans did not understand this, but most Americans did not speak fluent French and had little, if any, appreciation of foreign cultures. I had found that immersion in the culture of any host country is basic to work as an intelligence officer, and usually leads to professional benefits because it encourages locals to trust one.

Trust is as important to the intelligence professional as cynicism, maybe more important. Trust and cynicism are the *yin* and *yang* of the craft. Sooner or later, everybody needs a friend. Sooner or later, intelligence officers need cynicism.

Poor Kozlov. He was the representative of a rapidly declining totalitarian dictatorship that was approaching a total dead end. How could he not know this? The KGB was enormously powerful, both inside and outside the Soviet Union. The boys and girls at Lubyanka and Yasenevo were also smart and highly capable. In many ways their ruthlessness gave them considerable advantages over the CIA. I had worked against them my entire career and had developed professional if not admiring respect for them. What I did not understand was how such demonstrably intelligent people could support the corrupt Soviet regime. Maybe it had something to do with the Russian soul. Many would say it had something to do with cynicism and fear.

But that would be unfair to the Russians who have Russian reasons for what they do. Hell, most of them probably believed in Communism. God knows they've sacrificed terribly in its name. Sure, they were rational and no doubt recognized the faults of their system. The rampant corruption of the Brezhnev era was recognized even inside the USSR. But Russians could be patriots, too. And besides, aside from the Nomenklatura, the KGBniks were the elite of Russian society. It's nice to be part of the elite. Ironically, their greatest reward was the privilege of going abroad. Maybe that was enough for the KGBniks.

It required about a half-hour of purposeful strides to reach the neo-classical pile of stone that was the American Embassy. It was the last building to be erected on the *Place de la Concorde* in the 1930's, but it had been built to look much older so as to blend in with the surrounding architecture. I entered the marbled foyer, flashed my i.d. at the Marine Security Guard and headed for the elevator to the Agency spaces.

Eileen, the secretary for the front office gave me a reproachful look when I entered. "Where have you been? We called the restaurant, but they said you had left a half-hour ago."

Eileen was an attractive middle-aged blonde who was always well turned out. The plum assignment to Paris was probably her last overseas assignment after a long career. It was common knowledge that not only was she highly competent, but also that she was the long-time mistress of the current European Division Chief at Langley. She thus knew no fear and considered herself a full-fledged member of Station management. In fact, her competence was highly valued. The Division Chief had good taste.

"I decided to walk back. It's a nice day out there. 'April in Paris' and all that. Has something come up?"

"We don't know, but they've been calling for you at the *Place des Saussaies*. The boss says you should get over there pronto."

One of my duties was liaison with the French services, and No. 2 *Place des Saussaies* was the headquarters of the internal security service, the *Dirección de Surveillance du Territoire*, the DST. We usually met on Mondays, and an urgent call from the DST was unusual.

"OK. Can you call and tell them I'm on my way? It shouldn't take more than 15 minutes."

I reversed course and once outside set off around the corner to the *Boissy d'Anglas* that ran north-south along the side of the Embassy across the street from the ritzy *Hotel de Crillon*. A chef there long ago had invented eggs benedict. I could afford the eggs, but a single night's lodging there would consume a week's pay.

One block north was the *Faubourg Ste. Honoré*, sort of the Rodeo Drive of Paris, and just a couple of more blocks north and west lay the *Place des Saussaies*. No. 2 was a curious, but perhaps logical location for an internal security service. During the German occupation of World War II, it had been the Paris headquarters of the Gestapo. The façade was composed of unappetizing, dirty, yellowing granite blocks. I felt a subliminal chill every time I entered the disreputable place with its long, dingy corridors and interior walls of cold, gray stone, and its ghosts.

Chapter 2

A Volunteer

I found my usual DST interlocutor, Jacques Picard, waiting in the sparsely furnished stone chamber that served for liaison meetings. At the journeyman level, the French are not much for fancy surroundings, leaning more toward the utilitarian. The room contained a battered wooden desk and several straight-backed wooden chairs. A green bottle of lightly effervescent *Badois* water and a couple of glasses stood beside a telephone on the desk. Sly, hooded eyes in the Machiavellian countenance of French president François Mitterrand suspiciously observed us from a photo on the wall behind the desk.

The election of a socialist to the French presidency five years earlier and his appointment of four communists to his cabinet had alarmed Washington, but at their first meeting Mitterrand had reassured President Ronald Reagan of his loyalty to the West. A study in perpetual contradiction, Mitterrand would, in fact, reveal himself to be a strong Atlanticist.

Picard was in his early 40's, medium height, and beginning to go a bit soft around the middle. His full head of thick, brown hair showed not a speck of gray. His green eyes radiated a lively curiosity and intelligence, shaded by Gallic caution. He came from a long line of clockmakers in the Seine-Maritime region of Haute-Normandie. That's probably why he was such a stickler for detail. His heritage also made him quite predictable.

Picard rose from behind the desk when I entered

and extended his hand. "Hello, Clint," he said.

I gritted my teeth at the standing joke. People insisted that I resembled the actor Clint Eastwood, something I did not see, and the fact that my name was Harry evoked chortles from certain people.

"C'mon, Jacques, please!"

"Maybe you prefer "Dirty Harry?""

The French, I observed for the thousandth time, had a perverse sense of humor. "Plain Harry will do just fine, thanks. Why am I here?"

Picard turned serious and retreated back behind the desk. I took a seat in front. "We might need some help," said the Frenchman.

This was rare. Usually it was the other way around. My interest was piqued. I raised my eyebrows and waited.

Picard cleared his throat and took a deep breath. "First, please understand that we wouldn't ask this of you if there were more time or another way." Gallic pride served, he continued, "We have an interesting volunteer, something right up your alley. It's a Russian case, of course."

That got my attention.

"He's KGB Line X."

"The volunteer is here in Paris?"

"He was assigned to Paris in the 70's. Now he's in Moscow. It's hard for us to run operations there. We're a counter-intelligence service, and by law we can't operate outside of France." DST in French stood for *Dirección de Surveillance du Territoire*, the Directorate for Territorial Surveillance, basically with the same mission as the FBI.

With a hint of regret in his voice, Picard

continued, "We don't have a representative in Moscow."

Of course, they didn't. I was beginning to sense the direction the conversation was heading.

"It's a tough environment," I said carefully. "Our guys are covered by blanket surveillance 24/7. They can't take a shit without the Russians counting how many squares of toilet paper they use."

Running an agent in Moscow without special training, considerable planning and back-up could prove disastrous to both agent and case officer, as we had discovered a few times in recent months.

I realized that Picard was still talking.

"About six months ago, he stuck a package in the hand of the wife of one of our trade representatives while she was shopping at G.U.M.," the Frenchman continued, referring to the volunteer. "It was crowded. Scared the crap out of her, but she kept her wits and stuck it in her shopping bag, so she says. She only got a glimpse of the fellow's back. When she got back to the Embassy she handed it over to her husband and swore she would never shop at G.U.M. again."

"God," I said, "it's always G.U.M.?"

"Apparently, everyone in Moscow eventually can be found there," observed Picard dryly.

The scenario was familiar, even common. Western diplomats in Communist countries were regularly accosted on the streets by people who wanted to hand them notes. Most of them were mentally unstable – the note writers, that is – usually paranoid schizophrenics. Some were provocations. But occasionally it was the real thing – a so-called "volunteer" with something important to offer. Vetting, achieving further contact and setting up communications was always tricky, because there was usually no good way to establish the volunteer's *bona fides* without running a considerable risk. So there was a mating ritual to observe. The good ones knew enough to provide a verifiable taste of what they had to offer in the initial message, as well as a means of re-contact, that as often as not proved to be unacceptable. If the volunteer were an intelligence professional, he would know the steps to the dance. I wondered if the DST knew the steps. Their job was internal security, not foreign intelligence.

"And how did this package arrive in your hands?"

The bottle of mineral water was cold, and I watched a drop of condensation begin to slide down its side, slowly at first but gathering speed as it neared the desktop. That's how long it took the Frenchman to answer.

Picard almost blushed. "The trade representative is one of our 'honorable correspondents.'"

An "honorable correspondent" was what the CIA might term a "co-optee," someone who voluntarily works with an intelligence service for purely patriotic or ideological reasons, usually an American, or in the DST's case, a French citizen. Such people are not trained intelligence officers. It just happens that their position might make them valuable in some way.

"Shouldn't you just hand this over to the DGSE?"

The DGSE was the French foreign intelligence outfit, but we mostly considered them to be assholes. They had not helped their reputation when in 1984 they scuttled a Greenpeace ship, "The Rainbow Warrior" in Auckland, New Zealand, where their two operatives had been promptly arrested. We also knew that the DGSE had no qualms about stealing American secrets. In fact, the French were probably the best practitioners of industrial espionage in the entire world.

Picard gave me a blank stare that confirmed that we shared a common opinion of the DGSE. When he didn't speak, I asked, "So what's in the note that makes you stand up and salute?"

Picard smiled slyly in his best imitation of Mitterrand.

"As I said, he claims to be Line 'X,' a Department 'T' officer."

"That's a dark area. We assume they're stealing high tech gear and Western weapons systems wherever they can find them." I was tempted to add 'just like the DGSE,' but I didn't.

"For one thing, he claims to know the identities of several KGB agents, including a penetration of *Al Sakir*, one of the damnedest weapons sales in history. It's ironic that they chose the Arabic word for dove for a weapons deal. What do you know about it, Harry?"

There was no secret about the deal. It had been public for a couple of years. "You mean the Saudi deal with the Brits?"

"Yes, I'm talking about the Saudi deal with the Brits. It's bad enough that they won the deal to sell weapons to the fucking Wahabis, but it's even worse if the Russians have it wired."

"Why don't you just go straight to MI-6? It's their interests that are at stake, it seems to me." I thought the answer would be that if the Brits were penetrated, going to them with the information could be a misstep.

But there was another reason, a very French

reason, of course.

"The problem," replied Picard "is that British Aerospace alone stands to make billions – that's with a 'B' – of pounds. You Americans gave the deal a green light because it would be politically unwise for the U.S. to be selling weapons to Arabs these days, and Downing Street is turning cartwheels with joy. The entire British establishment is on board. It's the biggest boost to the British defense industry in decades, and they are particularly pleased because they snookered us out of the running."

My ears perked up at this. It was well-known that the Brits had somehow beaten the French to the punch with the Saudis, but no one knew exactly how they had pulled it off. "So, you believe that even if the Brits were warned they wouldn't do anything that might risk the sale. But *you* would not mind risking the sale?"

Picard gave me one of those resigned, European smiles, the kind assumed when speaking to naive Americans. "Since the end of World War I the Middle East has been our sphere of influence, and we managed to hold our own there against the Russians, a role the Americans fail to appreciate, as usual. We fully expect you to screw it up and then ask us to help put things right again."

Warming to his self-appointed role of enlightener of the ignorant, Picard continued, "Iran is the most dangerous regime on the face of the planet. They have oil wealth, and they are fanatics. We think the Russians and others might even be helping them develop nuclear weapons."

I settled back and crossed my legs to hear him out. This was getting interesting. French officials weren't normally so forthcoming with their American friends unless they wanted something. I wished I could light the Montecristo that still nestled in my pocket.

The Frenchman forged ahead, "So, what do we have?" He ticked his points off on his fingers, "an ambitious Iran, and the Russians playing a dangerous losing game in Afghanistan. Thanks to the Americans' childish antipathy towards France, they refuse always to listen to our advice. I predict there will be hell to pay in the not too distant future."

He looked me full in the face, "And now we come to the Saudis. Do you think they can fail to be concerned? Do you think they can sit idly by and watch the Shiite Persians grow in strength and influence while the Russians attack in Afghanistan? Iran is the center of terror, and no less so for the Saudis than for the Western Powers and the Israelis. Right now, they're fully engaged in the war with Iraq, but sooner or later, they'll get back to their main goal.

"Hell, if I were a Saudi I'd be scared out of my *thobe*! Their economy is totally dependent on oil, and there are serious threats to the regime. What do they have by way of military hardware to counter a regional threat like Iran? I'll tell you: an aging fleet of British and American fighters. What the Saudis need is superior strike aircraft, capable of penetrating Iranian defenses, armed with air-to-ground missiles and radar countermeasures. I could give you a list of equipment they require for air superiority.

"The American Congress refused the President's request for authorization to sell the Saudis 48 F-15E "Strike Eagle" dual role fighters."

The F-15E was capable of fighting its way to the

target over long ranges, destroying enemy ground positions, and fighting its way back out – a perfect fit for Saudi needs, especially if accompanied by the awesome AGM-65 Maverick air-to-ground missiles. I knew that the President's request had been refused by Congress, thanks in large part to the lobbying activities of the powerful America-Israel Public Affairs Committee, AIPAC. *If it involves the Middle East, it always comes down to the Israelis and their allies where Washington is concerned.*

Picard continued. "So King Fahd was royally pissed off - pardon the pun. The damned Israelis could defy even the American President. So he was forced to look elsewhere. Despite existing defense contracts with the Brits, he was afraid they would follow the American example. So he turned to us. We, too, have a lot of defense agreements with the Saudis.

"We wanted them to buy the Mirage or Serge Dassault's Rafale fighter. Visits and demonstrations were arranged. The Royal Saudi Air Force established a special committee to handle the project. The committee was given the name *Al Saif*, the 'tip of the sword,' headed by an Air Force General who also happens to be the son of the Saudi Defense Minister. Negotiations were well underway, but then the Saudis tossed a monkey wrench into the works – they wanted to pay in oil. We didn't like this. We know that Saudi finances are not what they used to be. Within a month, it all turned to *merde*. Our guys suddenly couldn't even get a meeting with the Saudi Defense Minister.

"Out of the blue, while our guys were still dithering about the method of payment, King Fahd announced his decision to purchase British Tornado aircraft, and we were completely frozen out. Nobody knows what happened to change the King's mind. We were screwed. The Brit deal is known as *Al Sakir*. It's the biggest goddamned arms deal in history.

"And that, Monsieur Harry, is where we stand today," concluded Picard. "The fact that our source in Moscow claims a Russian spy in London is deeply involved in the planning for *Al Sakir* is very interesting to France. I'm sure you understand. There are literally billions of francs in play here."

I was pretty sure the French thought they had found a way to screw the Brits. The question was, what did they expect us to do?

Picard was watching me closely. "We'd like the CIA to meet the volunteer in Moscow. We're offering you a joint operation in exchange for a little help."

Actually, it sounded like they wanted a lot of help.

Chapter 3

The joys of April in Paris temporarily forgotten, I returned to the Embassy feeling if not like Gene Kelly dancing in the street, still pretty good about being an American in Paris. I didn't exactly skip along the sidewalk, but the spook juices always start flowing in a strong current when an extraordinary operational opportunity presents itself. But this was a tricky one because of the British angle. The Brits were America's closest allies while the French were generally considered somewhat unreliable, especially by people in Washington who knew nothing about them. Hell, the frogs had elected a Socialist president, hadn't they? If Picard's story were true and they could actually tap a source inside Directorate 'T,' in all likelihood there would be a strong temptation to double-cross the French and tell the Brits. I wouldn't like it as a personal point of honor, but that kind of decision was above my pay grade and thus not a burden on my conscience. Did I mention that cynicism is a required trait for an intelligence officer?

Before I left, Picard had given me a file containing hard copies of some of the documents the volunteer had provided, clearly intended to serve as bait for us intel-hungry American spooks. There was a photo of the source's KGB i.d. card, as well. The documents were in English and contained technical specifications for what I took to be military equipment. What was worse, from the classification markings on them, the documents appeared to be American. According to the i.d. card, the volunteer's name was Barsikov and he held the rank of Lieutenant Colonel.

The explanation of why the source had turned to the French rather than the Brits, or even better, us, was pretty clear. He had been assigned to Paris under cover of the Soviet Trade Mission a decade earlier. The guy was a Francophile. There's no accounting for taste. But there was probably something more, maybe something he hadn't told his French buddies about.

Back in the Station spaces, I stopped by my office and instructed my secretary to run an immediate name trace on Barsikov before heading to the office of Chief of Station Terrence Stoddard, who looked up from the papers on his desk at the interruption. "You look like a man on a mission," he said.

Stoddard was several years older than me, and truth be told he was a sort of role model. He had sandy hair and an Errol Flynn moustache. At 57 he ran five miles every day which accounted for his trim figure. He'd graduated from Harvard in 1954 with a degree in French literature, and rumor had it that he preferred to read only in French. His brown tweed suit hung elegantly from his frame. He was a man who would look more in place in a private British men's' club or hosting a table at the *Tour d'Argent* than in the alleys where intelligence battles were fought.

"We need to talk," I said. "Do you have a few minutes?"

I looked at my watch. It was 4:30 PM, which meant it was still morning in Washington. I was certain we'd be writing a flash precedence cable this afternoon.

Stoddard rose and gestured at the grouping of a leather sofa and matching chairs at the opposite end of the spacious, wood-paneled office. The room boasted a brick fireplace, a reminder of more genteel times. Stoddard took a chair, crossed his legs, and waited for me to speak.

When I had finished, he sat back and steepled long fingers under his chin, his eyes focused in the distance as he digested the news.

"We're running traces now," I told him. "I put immediate Eyes Only precedence on it, so we should have something by tomorrow morning, but you might want to send the full story right now via flash. It'll light a fire under Soviet/East European Division."

"You're the Soviet expert, Harry. What are your preliminary thoughts?"

Stoddard had spent most of his career cultivating Middle Eastern potentates and was one of those rare bosses who knew when to rely on his subordinates.

I gathered my thoughts before speaking. "It's really too early to say. All volunteers are suspect, and the smart guys know this. The real deal will include probative information in the original approach, stuff that can be checked, and we don't know if Picard gave us the entire package. We've not vetted the info yet, but the French are no slouches. There are some American documents in the package he gave me, and if I don't miss my guess, they want to trade whatever the volunteer knows about penetrations of American programs for help getting the skinny on KGB involvement in *Al Sakir*."

I thought I was right about this, but the situation was complicated. "Any ops act in Moscow carries tremendous risk and usually requires weeks, maybe months of planning and site casing. Our officers there are under almost round the clock surveillance. In

Moscow you're playing on the enemy's turf, and they control it completely. In other words, the potential gain of an action has to be measured against the risk. According Picard, they don't have an officer in Moscow, and they don't want to hand this over to the DGSE. That's why they need us – to do the dirty work."

Stoddard nodded. "And the political equities?"

"This is the first time the French have asked us to work a source with them, and being French they can't resist chunking a stone at the Brits, hence the emphasis on the *Al Sakir* thing."

"French noses were put out of joint when they lost *Al Sakir* to the UK. It was unexpected, and they lost billions of dollars."

"They must realize that sooner or later, the Brits will have to be told."

"Perhaps, but there may well be American equities at risk that will make it all worthwhile, even if the French want to exact a price."

"They're not going to retrieve *Al Sakir* for themselves."

"They know that, but they have something in mind, even if it's only to embarrass *perfide Albion*."

"I'll start writing up the meeting for Langley."

"Of course. Photocopy the documents and we'll get a courier off tonight, as well."

Yeah, this was a big deal, a really big deal.

Chapter 4

My wife, Kate, and I had been assigned a roomy mansard apartment on the *Rue Godot de Mauroy* behind the *Place de la Madeleine*. The square was dominated by the Church of Sainte-Marie-Madeleine, said to have been dedicated to the glory of Napoleon's army. It looked more like a Roman temple to pagan gods than a Catholic church.

The apartment was ancient and drafty, but it featured carved wood wainscoting, multiple working fireplaces with marble mantels, creaking plank floors in a herringbone pattern, and floor to ceiling windows that opened over the rooftops of Paris. Drafty it may have been, but Kate loved it, and we had decided we would save no money during this tour in favor of spending it all on antiques, food, and exploring. Kate rationalized this decision with the idea that some people spend their entire lives without even seeing Paris, or they visit for only a short time, while she and I had at least three years to luxuriate in the frothy richness of it all. We needed to make some memories, Kate said. I, of course, agreed. I always agreed with her.

Kate had been with me through some tough assignments before Terrence Stoddard had chosen me for this plum posting. She deserved some fun. I could understand not wanting to waste it. I also liked the fact that I could walk to work amid some of the world's most impressive architecture.

After drafting and redrafting a cable report on the meeting with Picard and making sure a courier was headed to the airport with a diplomatic pouch containing Barsikov's original documents, I sauntered along *Rue de Rivoli* feeling pretty good about my day and glad that the big decision about running a risky op in Moscow had been laid at Langley's feet. I'd been part of such decisions in the past and each had been a balancing act trading off risk against potential gain. It was not at all the "game" some liked to call it. It was dead serious business with emphasis on the "dead."

In fifteen minutes I was home riding the tiny gilded cage that served as a lift up to the apartment. I would, of course, tell Kate everything. We were a team like most Agency couples.

Before I could open the apartment door, fearsome barking erupted behind it, and when I opened it, a black Scots Terrier danced in circles around my feet.

"Angus is ready for his walk." Kate's voice rang out from the kitchen.

"Angus can wait a few minutes. Don't I get to see you first?"

"You're early. C'mon in here and see what I got us from *Fauchon's* this afternoon. Oh, and I visited that wonderful *fromagerie* that just opened on the other side of the square. You just gotta go there with me next time. You're not gonna believe it. Imagine hundreds of cheeses. Oooh, the aromas!"

I followed her voice into the kitchen and grabbed my blond wife from behind and buried my face in the hair at the nape of her neck inhaling her scent. There was a pile of wrapped delicacies on the kitchen table that my practiced eye valued at several hundred francs.

"I found a really good *Pont l'Eveque*, your favorite." She wriggled from my grasp and handed me a knife directing my gaze to the small square wooden box containing the soft, pungent cheese. Grab a cracker and try it."

"I had a really big lunch today, hon. You're not planning to eat all of this stuff tonight, are you?"

"No. This is for a picnic this week-end. I thought we'd go to Compiègne Saturday and spend the night at that little *auberge* with the one-star restaurant. We can sign the register as *"Monsieur et Madame DuPont"* and pretend we're having an illicit affair. You can call me Fifi."

"And you can call me Gaston. I like the sound of that. The food's good there, too." We had become complete devotees of *Le Guide Michelin.*

"So, what do we do tonight? You're not hungry?"

"It's nice outside. It's April in Paris. Let's take Angus and go share a *plateau de fruits de mer* at that place near the opera. You can fill up, and I can just pick."

"A delightful idea, *Monsieur DuPont.*" She started shoving her purchases into the fridge. "So, how did your day go?"

I couldn't wait to tell her.

I still hadn't lit the Montecristo.

I arrived at the office early next morning, grabbed a *café au lait* and a fat, buttery croissant in the basement cafeteria, and headed straight for the comm shack to get the front office morning traffic. The cables were stacked in order of precedence, and on top was an immediate cable response from Langley to my report on

Barsikov. Kind of Headquarters to send it via immediate precedence rather than flash which would have awakened me in the middle of the night.

No one else was in so I lit my morning cigar and sat at my desk to read Langley's response.

I read it three times, then leaned back in the chair as far away from the document as I could get, as though it emitted an offensive odor. My cigar lay forgotten and dead in an ashtray. Had anyone been there to read my expression, they would have described it as gobsmacked.

Through the door, I heard someone enter the office suite and hoped it was Terrence Stoddard. We had a lot to talk about.

Chapter 5

I handed the cable to Stoddard and plopped heavily onto the leather sofa.

Reading my expression, Stoddard said, "It's a little early in the morning to be so pissed off, Harry. You usually don't reach this point until sometime after noon."

"I can't wait to see your reaction to this." I thrust the HQS cable in his direction. "And to think I had begun to like the French."

Stoddard assumed a bland expression and took a seat beside me before plucking his reading glasses from his pocket and turning his attention to the three-page cable. About half-way through the first page, his eyebrows began to travel up his forehead. When he finished reading he puffed out his cheeks and blew air through his lips.

He looked at me over the tops of his half-moon reading glasses. "The French like to hedge their bets," he said, "and politics is a game they like to play. I guess we shouldn't be surprised."

"Well," I snorted, "I'm sure as hell surprised, not to mention pissed off. They went right around us. According to that cable, Picard's boss, the Director of the DST, travelled to Washington, without telling us as protocol demands, and met with the Vice President of the United States. This happened two days ago, and no one at Headquarters thought to let us know."

"They know one another from the time the VP was the DCI," said Stoddard, referring the DST chief and the Vice President. "There's a personal relationship there, and to the French that's always the preferred route because it means leverage."

"And he tells the Vice President the same thing Picard told me about the volunteer. Why did Picard even take the time?"

"It's probably their idea of professional courtesy." I thought the Chief of Station might be kidding.

I snorted again. In direct contrast to the way I was feeling the day before, I had now revised my opinion of the French downward. "It's more like a professional joke, and I'm the butt of it."

"You have every right to be angry, but it's out of our hands now. Washington made the decision for us."

"You mean the White House put pressure on Langley, and Langley caved."

"We work for the White House. And maybe the French argument was convincing."

"So now we have politicians making intelligence decisions?"

"Thus has it ever been, and you should know it. Politics usually trumps everything else." He was right. When all was said and done, the people who really ran Washington inhabited 'K' Street, not the White House or Capitol.

"And it's my ass on the line."

"You can always refuse. I'll back you if that's what you decide."

The look on Stoddard's face told me he meant it despite the precarious political position in which it would place him. "You know I can't do that and remain with the Agency. I don't think even you could win an argument with the White House."

Stoddard leaned toward me, elbows on the desk.

"I don't like it any more than you."

"I know. But if I make it out of this alive, I'm going to kick Picard's hairy frog ass." I probably wouldn't, but it made me feel better to say it.

It was the third page of the HQS cable that bothered me most. Langley had decided that Moscow Station should not be involved on the grounds that personnel were few and the operations they were currently running were too important for them to risk one of their case officers, at least that's what the cable said. That argument had resonated at Langley. Even a White House order had to be balanced against the integrity of the most important operations the Agency was running anywhere. But a White House order was a White House order. So a compromise was proposed. Sending me to Moscow to make the meeting was the compromise. Although I had never been to Moscow, a previous successful tour in Eastern Europe meant that I had the requisite denied area experience. I suppose I should have been flattered that Langley wanted to put my ass on the line.

Stoddard was thinking along the same lines. "You have the necessary training and experience. That's something."

"Damn it," I said, "There are guys at Headquarters who have served in Moscow and know the turf. I don't know the turf, and that means I'll have a snowball's chance in hell of spotting surveillance."

"Maybe. But anyone who has served there previously would be known to the Seventh Directorate," said Stoddard, referring to KGB surveillance in Moscow. "The risk would be even higher. And for the time being Langley and the French want to keep this on a need to know basis for obvious reasons."

He continued, "And there's something else, Harry. Reading between the lines, I don't think Langley is telling us everything. It takes something pretty big to tempt them into something as risky as this. You'd better go home and get packed for a flight to Washington. We'll reserve a seat for you on this afternoon's United flight to Dulles. I'll have Eileen make the reservations."

"Thanks. I hope they have an adequate supply of scotch on board." The week-end plans with Kate disappeared like a popped soap bubble.

Chapter 6

Langley

Kate was disappointed about cancelling plans for Compiègne but more worried about the job ahead. I explained everything to her, of course, and if anything she was angrier than I. There was just time to throw a couple of changes of clothing into a carry-on bag and get to Charles DeGaulle Airport. Eileen had arranged for me to receive VIP treatment and a Business Class seat, and I was whisked through security and boarded with time to spare.

There was lots of time on the long flight to think. This was obviously a big deal. But it could just as easily be a provocation. Why was Washington so hot to trot?

The plane touched down at Dulles in mid-afternoon, right on time. I rented a car and took the Dulles Access Road to the beltway and turned south toward the American Legion Bridge, finally taking the exit to the George Washington Parkway and the Headquarters entrance a few miles further.

Spring was treating the Metro area well, and the dogwood trees on the Langley campus were in white and pink bloom. The gate guard had been advised of my arrival, and handed me a pass to park in the VIP lot at the front of the building. The courtesy did not cheer me in the least.

Alongside the main entrance, the larger than life statue of Nathan Hale bravely awaiting the gallows with his hands tied behind his back did not cheer me either. Sure, he was a hero, but he'd been caught by the British with a secret message hidden in his shoe. He needed more training.

I wondered what the basement of Lubyanka was like.

I headed straight for the front office of the Soviet/East European Division, said hello to Sadie Cochran, the Division Chief's perennial secretary, as I strode past her into Barton Graham's office. Graham, the division Chief, had returned from a stint as Chief of Station, Moscow only two years earlier. He was tall and thin with dark hair receding across a prominent brow. Graham was renowned for his sharp intelligence and acerbic tongue. He looked more like a college professor than a spook, and he didn't suffer fools lightly.

Graham looked up from a stack of cables over the tops of a pair of black, horn-rimmed glasses. "Harry, you don't look happy."

"Fact is, Barton, I just got off of a nine hour flight going in the wrong direction and I'm pissed off at Headquarters. And by 'Headquarters,' I mean you."

I sat without waiting for an invitation facing Graham's large wooden, Government Issue desk and glared at the Division Chief.

"You can thank your French friends, not Headquarters." His voice was neutral and unconcerned. If he was concerned about my opinion, he didn't show it.

"What the fuck do we have a Moscow Station for if they can't be tasked with an op on their own turf?" Nothing like getting straight to the point. "Don't tell me that wasn't a Headquarters decision, your decision."

"You're right. The decision was made, and you'll just have to live with it." Graham was not a man to mince words.

"Can you share the rationale?"

Graham hesitated a few beats and scowled. "All I can tell you is that the Station has some problems we're struggling to understand. We've lost some assets there recently."

"So does that mean you don't trust anyone in the Station, that you suspect poor tradecraft is at fault, or something worse? I hope you have a good reason for dropping me into that soup. "

I received a stare from Graham that said I was stupid and unworthy to be a CIA officer and that he always had a good reason for what he did. Its effect was to make the object of his disdain feel guilty for venturing an opinion. "Neither the quality of the decision to send you nor the reason is for you to judge. The decision was made by people with considerably more knowledge than you. It was not taken lightly. What we expect of you is to do the job you're given. No one thinks it will be easy."

He closed his eyes for a moment, as though to shut the odious vision of me out of his sight.

But as it turned out, he was making a decision to take me at least a little further into his confidence.

"I will tell you two things that should settle the matter once and for all. That classified American document the volunteer provided contained the specifications for the territorial defense radar system that protects the United States, the Defense Early Warning system, or DEW line. Apparently, the KGB knows everything there is to know about it. We don't think the KGB would give up that sort of information, so it's a strong substantiation of the volunteer's *bona fides*. Secondly, the volunteer appears to be an intelligence officer and claims to know the identities of KGB agents and sources."

The second point was important because written large in the Graham canon was the conviction that that the Russians would never, ever dangle an intelligence officer to be recruited by us. I didn't necessarily agree, but no one was going to resurrect the Nosenko case to rebut the Division Chief.

Graham continued, "Given what has been happening with Moscow Station, we are anxious to see what he has. Now stop being appalled by Headquarters decisions and get to work. Sadie has the details for you."

So they hoped the volunteer would shed some light on the problems of Moscow Station. That was more than enough to encourage Graham to toss me to a pack of hungry Russian wolves.

He bent back to his cables and waved me, now open mouthed in amazement, out of the office. As I stepped through the door still shaking my head, the Division Chief called out, "Good luck, Harry. I know you'll get the job done. And, by the way, you are to have no contact with Moscow Station."

That was Barton Graham - slap you around, call you an idiot, rub your face in the dirt, then pat you on the back and give you more bad news. I suspected the man was a sadist. But deep down, I admired him as a professional's professional whose confidence and trust I valued. Did that make me a masochist? Of course not.

Well, maybe. I did work for the CIA.

I'd learned two important facts and drawn a clear inference from the conversation. First, Langley had serious doubts about the security of Moscow Station. Second, Barsikov was the source of a document that scared the striped pants off of Washington. And the inference was that the wily frogs were using the value of the intel to force Langley to take the risk of running an unorthodox and dangerous operation in the heart of the Evil Empire. And then there was Picard's emphasis on *Al Sakir*. I had a feeling I hadn't heard the last of the arms deal, but as far as Washington was concerned this was small potatoes compared to what we might gain. I couldn't argue that point.

The first stop after Graham was the Reports section where I found the Division's Chief reports officer, Jerry Markham, waiting. He was drinking a cup of coffee when I entered and pointed in the direction of a coffee maker on the credenza behind his desk. There were several heavy, Navy style mugs alongside it. I poured myself a cup which I hoped would keep me alert. We sat at a small table with the door closed.

The angular, white haired Markham was an old Soviet hand. All Soviet and East European reporting passed through his hands before the analysts ever saw it. Everything the Agency knew about the USSR was in his head. To my surprise, he started with *Al Sakir*. I had no choice but to play along.

"We've pulled together every piece of information available on the arms deal. Much of the press reporting is repetitive, but the British left wing newspapers and anti-war wingnuts, especially *The Guardian*, have done a good job digging up dirt. With a Tory at No. 10 Downing Street they're doing their best to cause the Government trouble. That aside, it's been difficult for our military attachés to dig out much insider information, although there are a couple of interesting leads to follow.

"What is clear from the press is that everyone suspects there is a massive amount of corruption associated with the deal. We're talking hundreds of millions of dollars here. The Saudi Government, if you can call it that, allegedly insists on paying using a barter arrangement with so-called "Princes' oil" rather than cash, something at which the French balked. But the Brits are keeping a tight lid on the actual modalities. Barter arrangements leave a lot of room for finagling around the edges. Someone in London obviously saw an opportunity when the French hesitated and took advantage of it. The primary suspect is a wealthy Saudi who has resided in the UK for many years and is married to a Brit. His name is Wafiq al Salah. He owns several expensive homes including a large house in central London. He's very well-known and very well liked because of his charitable activities. He's also donated large amounts to the Tory Party. *The Guardian* has him pegged as the primary go-between for the Brits with the Saudis. He apparently is very close to his cousin, the Saudi Defense Minister."

I asked, "Who are the players on the British side?" *It was among the Brits that a Russian agent was most likely to be found, given past history.*

"The Prime Minister, of course, is a strong supporter, and there are few who can stand up to her. Regardless of personalities, this arms sale represents a gargantuan boost to the British defense industry, especially British Aerospace. It's hard to see how anyone on their side of the Channel would be against it, except for the peacenik lefties, of course." Markham smiled thinly. "And Washington is a strong supporter, too. We would be making the sale ourselves if we could."

Of course, we would. How the hell had Congress resisted the blandishments of the arms industry's 'K' Street lobbyists, the front men for the Military-Industrial complex? AIPAC carried surprising clout; also, I suspected influence over a hefty number of campaign contributors. "OK. It's to be expected that the British Government would work hard to make the deal happen. British Aerospace is the crown jewel of their defense industry. Who else is involved besides the PM?"

"At the working level there are two: the head of the Tornado sales program at British Aerospace, Jeffrey Spade, and the Minister of State for Defense Procurement, James Abbott. Abbott has been in and out of trouble for years, even accused of violating the Official Secrets Act a few years ago, but he always manages to come out smelling like a rose. According to the Embassy, he's well plugged-in to some high level Middle Eastern types in the UK, too."

This guy sounded like a prime candidate to be a Soviet mole.

"Does Abbot have a relationship with Al Salah?"

"No. That would not have escaped public attention. It's someone else, but someone who works hard to stay off the radar."

"According to the French, Barsikov provided the

identities of several KGB sources in his initial package, as well as information that should lead to the identification of others. There is no doubting the counterintelligence value." He took a sip of coffee before continuing. "Did Barton tell you about the Moscow Station problems?"

"Yes."

He shook his head and turned gloomy. "The volunteer promised to dig into *Al Sakir*, obviously to get the French interested. He's clever and is probably somewhat of a Francophile. But I'm sure you understand why we are interested, too. Regardless of the reason the French approached us, I believe the vast majority of the documents this source could provide concern the security of the United States. We are the 'main enemy,' after all. For once, the French are acting like good allies. Second, they have a dogged interest in *Al Sakir*. There may be a price we'll have to pay in that regard for the information, and that's why I'm telling you about it. But all we can do now is wait and see what comes of your meeting."

He paused for a moment as though he were chewing over a decision. "Barton is quite worried. We have some pretty big national equities at stake here, too."

"I know. Barton told me."

"There was another document in the package, a British document. It contained the schematics for a look down/shoot down radar we had sold to the Brits."

Well, here was another reason Washington was sending me to Moscow. Interesting, if the Brits were including American origin systems in the *Al Sakir* deal, at least some US contractors had their finger in the pie

despite Congressional disapproval.

Chapter 7

Moscow

Landing at Sheremetyevo Airport was an almost surrealistic experience. When the plane finally taxied to a stop on the tarmac a squad of uniformed guards with AK-47's trotted out to surround it. They didn't look friendly. For an instant I wondered if this was a welcoming committee just for me but just as quickly discarded the notion. This was, after all, the heart of the Evil Empire, and armed guards should be no surprise.

The passengers deplaned down some spindly flight stairs that had been wheeled up to the hatch accompanied by more armed guards. The smell of jet fuel from the tarmac was overpowered as soon as we entered the terminal by an atmosphere charged with antiseptic cleaning fluid mixed generously with body odor. I headed for the line waiting at the diplomatic passport control, but it looked just as long and glum as the one for regular travelers.

I had expected to fly to Moscow directly from Washington, but yet again I found myself the victim of a tightly held deal between the White House and Langley on one side and the DST on the other. I'd returned to Paris where Picard helpfully supplied an alias French diplomatic passport. Ironically, the name they gave me was "Pierre DuPont." Kate got a perverse kick out of that. The alias was the French equivalent of "John Smith." Langley had fitted me with a light disguise that consisted of a brush cut, black, horn rimmed glasses, and snap on false teeth that combined to give me the appearance of a near-sighted horse. The clothes I wore were a size too large to disguise my build. I was feeling more and more like Langley's redheaded stepchild. With a French identity there was no way Langley could intervene if things went wrong.

An hour and a half later I was still in the same line wishing I'd taken advantage of the rest room facilities on the plane before landing. The good news was that there were only two people left in line ahead of me.

When my turn finally came I was confronted by a hostile young man in a rumpled, brown uniform with shoulder boards I couldn't identify. I guess the only thing more tedious that waiting in line was a job that consisted of delaying the progress of the line as long as possible. He held out his hand for documents without even looking at me, studied the passport with all the disdain of an exterminator looking at a dead rat, and then looked up at me, back down at the passport, then again up at me. Then he picked up a phone that might have had a supporting role in a Hollywood movie of the 1930's, turned away and engaged in a hushed conversation with whoever was on the other end of the line. He might have been talking to his wife about the groceries he was to pick up on the way home for all I knew. On the other hand, he might have been telling his superiors that he had a guy with a lousy disguise at his counter and needed permission to shoot him. He finally replaced the handset and glared at me before grabbing a rubber stamp with which he struck an empty page of the passport with enough force to knock out Muhammed Ali. There might be a special training course for this skill. Welcome to the USSR.

Finally through passport control, I found my contact waiting in the main hall. This was Lucien Gagnon, the French trade representative whose wife had received the package from the volunteer. He was obviously glad to see me and led the way to a Peugeot sedan with a Russian driver just outside the terminal.

"Long flight, huh," said Gagnon. "First time in Moscow?" We spoke in French, of course.

"Yep." I wasn't in a conversational mood.

"Sit back and take in the view," said Gagnon, it's long way into town."

Fortunately, he was not the talkative type. This was probably due to the Russian driver.

Sheremetyevo is located outside the Moscow Ring Road, and we passed old wooden huts, known in Russian as *isbushki*, along the way. Many sported colorful wooden shutters, and some of the huts were slightly tilted, as though the foundation had settled on one side. There were weeds everywhere. Apparently the concept of the manicured lawn had found no place in dialectic materialism. Either that or the Russians were a bunch of drunken, lazy bastards. Maybe it all went together.

By the time we reached the Ring Road and penetrated the outskirts of Moscow proper we passed one gray, multi-story apartment building after another marching down both sides of the street. I concluded that the USSR might have been designed by the Salvation Army. The apartment buildings demonstrated an astounding lack of originality in the Soviet school of architecture. Chunks of masonry had fallen off many of the buildings, and laundry was hung out on the balconies.

It was gray, grim, and bleak. The gray was occasionally brightened up by the presence of large, red banners extolling the virtues of Communism. Obviously, it was imperative to remind the inmates of their good fortune.

The whole damned place would look better under about three feet of snow. That was the romantic view promoted by the commissars, happy commies freezing their asses off in teetering wooden huts with colorful shutters.

Seemed about right.

My ruminations about the future of Communism were interrupted by Gagnon. "We'll drop you off at your hotel. We got you a room at the Metropol. It's not far from Red Square, so you can take in the sights."

"The sights are pretty depressing."

"Oh, the Kremlin at night is impressive. When there's snow, it's like a fairy tale."

"Maybe a Grimm fairy tale." Disneyland it most definitely was not. My thoughts strayed back to lunch with Kozlov only a few days ago. Was it Kozlov's dream to turn Paris into another Moscow? How the hell could a rational human being fail to note the contrast?

There wasn't a lot of traffic, even after entering the city proper. Foreign made vehicles were few and far between. It was all all Zhigulis, Volgas, Pobedas, and the occasional Zaporozhets. Every once in a while a Chayka or Zil limousine would zoom down the middle of the street with a police escort.

"Four legs good; two legs bad." The famous slogan from Orwell's "Animal Farm" kept circling in my

head.

Chapter 8

Kolomenskiy Park

I didn't want to think too much about whether the French impersonation was intended to protect Langley or to protect me. Barton Graham felt he could not trust Moscow Station, and that had all sorts of nasty implications. Had the KGB somehow penetrated the Station? Could there be a mole at Headquarters? Some important Moscow operations had been compromised. Everybody was worried. What worried me was that I could not count on Agency back-up. In fact, I wasn't sure I could trust Barton Graham. I didn't really trust the French, and I sure as hell didn't trust the Russians.

Back at Langley the existence of the operation was closely held. Maybe only four or five people knew the details, including the DCI. Of course, there was also the White House to consider, and the White House was not the greatest bastion of secrets, unless it was to conceal presidential skullduggery.

Gagnon treated me to dinner that evening in the restaurant in my hotel. He had earlier suggested that I come to his apartment for a proper meal, but I thought staying off the streets for the time being was a good idea. He shrugged and reluctantly agreed. We sat at our table for a good half-hour before a less than interested waiter wearing a greasy black jacket and less than snow-white shirt shuffled up to take our order.

Gagnon said such a delay was normal in Moscow. He advised me to ignore the menu and asked the waiter what was available. The surly waiter looked as though he couldn't care less and unenthusiastically recommended *kuropatka*. Partridge sounded OK to me, but Gagnon only smiled ruefully and asked for a plate of pickled herring and bread. He also ordered bottled water and vodka. It was the first time I had shared a table with a Frenchman who did not order wine.

The seemingly interminable wait between placing our order and the arrival of the food via the same dour-faced waiter provided ample time to talk.

Gagnon was quite nonchalant and cheerful. Easy for him. He repeated what Picard had told me in Paris. There was no tension between the Soviets and the French. The French had long ago ceased trying to run intelligence operations in Moscow, a fact of which the Russians were aware. As a consequence, he breezily assured me, no one at the French Embassy or Trade Mission was ever subjected to surveillance. I received this with a grain of salt large enough to choke a frog, and there were several frogs I could envision choking.

When the food finally arrived, I was presented with a plate containing a few boiled potatoes, a messy green sludge that might at one time have been canned asparagus, and the *kuropatka*. The *piece de resistance* was a tiny shriveled bird with decorative white paper booties on its feet. There was no discernable meat on the mummified carcass.

I pushed the plate aside, and Gagnon, with an 'I told you so' smirk, suggested we share the pickled herring and black bread. It went well with the vodka, which was good.

Contact was to take place the next day, and I hoped to get an early start. But there was a grim looking middle-aged woman at a desk in the corridor outside my room whose job it was to note the movements of guests and probably give a signal when it was all clear for a KGB team to search a room. It would be suspicious to try to sneak out before dawn. There was no sneaking Russia. That left me with precious little time to determine whether I was being watched.

Then again, why would the KGB watch me when all they had to do was lay in wait at the rendezvous site? "The French are not surveilled in Moscow" became my mantra.

The volunteer's original note instructed to await contact at precisely 10:30 AM on a Saturday, just outside the entrance to the ancient Church of the Holy Ascension in Kolomenskiy Park, a short distance southeast of Moscow center and still within the city limits. The green expanse of the park stretched down to the banks of the Moscow River. Spring was slower in coming to Moscow, and it was chilly. The trees were just beginning to revive. It was a popular tourist area, dominated by the graceful white church, built in 1532. Such an open area made counter surveillance particularly difficult, but there was no alternative, and besides, French citizens were "never surveilled."

Of course not.

Barton Graham, a former Moscow Chief of Station, had briefed me on modes of transportation so I knew how to get to the rendezvous. I had heard a lot about the splendors of the Moscow subway. But what I experienced was a herd of irritated Muscovites jostling one another as they packed onto the train. I wondered if the Kremlin had considered weaponizing body odor.

Regardless of the time I spent "dry-cleaning" myself before arriving at the park, if this were a provocation it wouldn't make any difference anyway. They would be waiting for me here in a traditional KGB ambush. A bunch of heavyset guys would leap out of the bushes and wrestle me to the ground while another ground away with a video camera. I would be indelicately searched and tossed into the back of a van for the ride to Lubyanka.

The arrangements put the volunteer in the driver's seat, and I felt like a sitting duck.

As instructed I carried a G.U.M. shopping bag thoughtfully provided by Gagnon and wore a blue jacket as recognition signals.

Barsikov showed up right on time. He was easy to spot while he was still at some distance because he was making a bee-line directly toward me almost at a trot. He was tall and good-looking with a full head of jet black hair and droopy, arctic blue eyes that were fixed on me. He showed no signs of fear. Whether that was good or bad, I would soon find out.

The Russian halted and looked me up and down. "*Est que vous êtes un ami de Lucien?*" he asked.

"*Oui.*" If he preferred French, I was his guy.

He stared at me for a few beats more, then shrugged and said, "Let's go for a walk," before setting off in the direction of a wooded section of the park.

I didn't move, but instead asked to see his identification. "You are a good officer," he said with an appreciative smile, and produced his KGB identification card, the same one in the photo in his original package.

I looked around as we walked. There were a lot of people, mostly families taking advantage of the good weather for a week-end outing. No one seemed particularly interested in us.

Barsikov clutched a G.U.M. shopping bag in one hand which he thrust in my direction. "This is for you."

The bag was bulky but not heavy. Now that I had it in my hands was the time for the KGB to swoop in for the kill. I involuntarily tensed up in anticipation of some big, burly guys in trenchcoats grabbing me.

But no one did. *The French are not surveilled in Moscow.*

"How much time do you have?" I asked the standard case officer question.

Barsikov was completely relaxed. "As much as we need."

"No one knows you are here?" By this I mean did anyone else know what he was up to.

"No. Don't worry, and don't bother with such questions. We have as long as we need, and then it's over. You won't see me again."

"Why not?"

"I don't think I have much more time."

"I thought you said we had all the time we need."

"I mean me. I don't think that I personally have much time left."

This could mean anything. "Are you ill? Tell me about it."

He smiled wistfully, "I don't think I'm ill in any way you would understand. There's nothing to tell. That bag contains everything I could get my hands on. It took months, carrying documents out of Yasenevo every day and back the next. I cleaned out the important files. I think you will be especially interested in the *Al Sakir* information and the list of KGB assets in

France. It provides an opportunity."

"Why are you doing this?"

He grimaced and indicated a bench alongside the graveled path. "Let's sit down for a while." He suddenly looked very tired, like a runner at the end of a long distance race.

He said he was an engineer, a good one, and that he had landed in a dead-end job at Yasenevo. All he saw was corruption and nepotism all around him. All the good jobs, the overseas postings went to the sons and associates of the *nomenklatura*. There was no place for merit in the Soviet system.

He leaned back on the bench and turned his face to the sun, his eyes closed, and expelled a long, ragged sigh. "I have nothing left to look forward to, and I wish for nothing more than to do as much damage as possible before the end."

"Would you like to come to France? It might be possible to arrange it." Picard had instructed me to make this proposal although I saw no way they could accomplish an exfiltration. I was also authorized to offer money. But this guy was the epitome of Russian fatalism.

He turned toward me with eyes that did not appear to see me. He was looking somewhere else, somewhere far away. "No. I don't want to leave Russia. This is my country, and I will stay here."

I waited for him to say more, but he didn't. Finally, he stood and held out his hand. "Thank you for coming. I wasn't sure you would, but I'm grateful. You won't see me again."

He was not interested in our plans for future contact, wouldn't even listen to me. He had his own agenda.

With that, he turned and strode away leaving me literally holding the bag.

The bag Barsikov gave me contained what looked like more than 100 roles of undeveloped film. If the documents he had included in his initial package were anything to go by, I was carrying potentially the most important intelligence haul ever acquired in the Soviet Union. My earlier concerns shoved aside, I headed straight for the hotel and called Lucien Gagnon from my room.

We had arranged that I would call him as soon as I returned to assure him all was well, i.e. that I was not hanging from my thumbs in the basement of Lubyanka. I'm damned if I know what they would have done had I not called.

I'd been turning everything over in my mind all the way back to the hotel and made a decision that probably wouldn't please anyone, either at Langley or in Paris. I know it seemed reckless. There was a small chance it would turn out to be disastrous. But I had my reasons, and I thought they were good ones.

I called Gagnon from my room. "I'm back in the hotel, Lucien, and I'm tired. I think I'll go to bed." This was our pre-arranged safety signal. I asked Gagnon to book a flight to Paris the following morning. The plan was for him to pick me up and drive to the Trade Mission if the meeting had been successful, but to get me out of Moscow immediately if Barsikov had not turned up at the rendezvous.

I had my reasons for stiffing the French. The way Picard and his boss had handled things still pissed me off. But that wasn't the most important reason, although I'll admit that the thought of a little subterfuge of my own was quite appealing. There was a stronger reason, and I hoped Langley would agree with me.

Judging from the documents the DST had shared with us, the Soviets had access to some pretty hairy American secrets. That was what Jerry Markham thought, and Jerry was a smart guy.

We had agreed with the DST that I would hand over to Gagnon whatever booty came from Barsikov for transmission to Paris via diplomatic courier. It had occurred to me early on that I could well be handing over to the French, who were notoriously proficient at stealing industrial secrets, a treasure trove of American secrets the Russians had managed to steal. The French, being French, would not hesitate to exploit such a bonanza for their own froggish ends. They would in all likelihood then share everything, or almost everything, with us, but they would control the exchange.

That did not sit well with me. After all, I was the one who had run all the risk. So why not hold onto the film and let Langley decide how to use it and what to share? After everything else, I figured there would be little risk getting the film back to Paris in the bottom of my carry-on bag. The diplomatic passport I carried should exempt me from baggage checks at the airport.

So I sat packed my bag and sat on it in my room all night like a hen hatching eggs.

I wondered if the French would declare me

persona non grata. Kate and I would miss Paris.

Chapter 9

Langley

Barton Graham was still staring at me mutely when I risked a sidewise glance in his direction. He might have been measuring me for a casket. I shrugged and finished my report, "He handed me the film cassettes in a bag and walked away into the sunset. Then I got out of Dodge, and here I am."

I'd returned to Washington after grabbing a quick change of clothes from home in Paris and stuffing the film into a diplomatic pouch. I'd spent about 24 hours either in the air or hanging around airports, and I was a little loopy. I should have stopped by the cafeteria for a cup of black coffee, but had made a bee line for Graham's office instead.

Not the best condition to confront a Division Chief with a *fait accompli*. I had been a naughty boy.

When I finished, Graham scowled at me for a few long, silent minutes before speaking. My return to Washington had been expected, of course, because Terry Stoddard and I had forewarned him.

Picard had made increasingly insistent telephone calls to the Station for me meet the DST as soon as possible, but I had ducked back out of the country without responding.

At last, Graham said. "So, all on your own, you decided to steal the French operation."

Obviously, I had done exactly that, but he expected some sort of answer, so I replied, "It's not entirely a French operation, is it? But, yes, and that kept a whole bunch of sensitive intelligence on the

United States out of French hands."

"You do realize that the Vice President gave his word on this."

"Once that film is developed and everyone here sees what's on it, there may be a change of opinion."

"The French are very upset about this."

"The French make a habit of being pissed off. It's a national pastime. I didn't see any sense in making them the beneficiaries of the KGB's hard work and letting them decide whether or not to share it. Now the decision is in our hands, and if the Vice President wants to hand it all to the French, he's free to do it. I doubt that he will, though."

"This could spoil our liaison relationship with the French. They turned to us precisely because they knew the bulk of the KGB intel would most likely concern the United States. It's why we accepted their proposal."

"That's true, Barton, but the DGSE has been stealing industrial secrets for decades, including American secrets. What kind of relationship is that?"

"An old and very valuable one."

My only hope was to stick to my guns, so I said, "There's another thing. When the DST briefed me it was very clear that besides uncovering moles in France, they had a real interest in what the Russian could tell them about the *Al Sakir* deal with the Brits. If there is relevant information on the film, it should go a long way toward softening them up."

Graham was angry but holding it in, something for which I was grateful. His white hot rages were infamous for reducing people to tiny, bleeding pieces of meat. There should have been a nurse on duty in the

SE front office to take care of his victims.

"Go away, Harry. I don't want to see you for a while, not until we've analyzed the film and decided what to do." He glared at me in a way that should have melted the lenses of his glasses.

People in positions like Graham's do not like decisions taken out of their hands. They want to be in control, sometimes for good reasons, sometimes for bad ones. But Barton Graham was at heart an operations officer who could appreciate independent initiative – so long as the result was positive. I hoped that in the end, he would come down on my side. If not, I could be flipping burgers at MacDonalds in a few weeks.

Chapter 10

London

Wafiq al Salah stared at his reflection in the mirror as he wiped the remainder of the shaving cream from his jaw with a soft, white hand towel. At 38, he was still boyishly handsome, though his face was marred by a flattened nose, a permanent souvenir from a terrible experience in his youth. He had never had his appearance cosmetically restored because the broken nose reminded him daily to avoid making foolish decisions.

He splashed on some cologne and finished dressing. The meeting this morning was important and a fine bespoke suit had been laid out by the maid. Satisfied with the way he looked in the dressing room's full length mirror, he descended the elegantly curved staircase to the foyer of his Knightsbridge house just south of Hyde Park. His wife, still in her dressing gown emerged from the morning room to look him over.

"Darling, you look splendid," she said. Becky Haversham al Salah was from a wealthy West Country family, and she dearly loved her dashing Arab husband. He was to her mind wise and mature beyond his age. Over the years he had become quite "westernized" in both manner and outlook and through dint of wise investments and knowing how to take advantage when opportunity knocked, Wafiq had amassed a huge fortune in an incredibly short amount of time.

To people, especially women, who did not know him, he seemed deliciously dark and mysterious, always charming and sophisticated. He was well known as a philanthropist, a man who took an interest in current events, as well as a connoisseur of fine horseflesh. Although he owned residences in New York, Paris, Houston, Los Angeles, and Riyadh, London was his home base.

"So," he asked his wife, "do I pass inspection. Will they let me through the door at 10 Downing Street?"

Among Wafiq's many interests was politics, and he was a stalwart contributor to Tory Party causes. This guaranteed access to the halls of British power when he needed it. Over several years he had developed an especially cordial relationship with the current Prime Minister. She had summoned him to a meeting this morning.

"Wafiq," replied Becky, "*Any* woman would be pleased to see you grace her door, even the Prime Minister."

Becky was inordinately proud of him and appreciated his always considerate nature. She had given him two children, a girl and a boy, still in their pre-teens, and she knew he was content with her. Most importantly, he was a good man.

Wafiq's chauffeur opened the door of the Bentley when the Saudi descended the front steps to the courtyard, and after ensuring that his charge was comfortable in the rear seat with the morning papers, slid behind the wheel. The heavy car glided silently from the curved drive into the street.

Fifteen minutes later the Bentley pulled to a stop at the large wrought iron gates that had been installed at the end of Downing Street following an IRA mortar attack on the Prime Minister's residence a few years ago. The shells had missed the structure entirely and landed in a back yard, blowing out some windows. Wafiq was uncertain about exactly how wrought iron gates might impede a mortar attack.

A security officer greeted him as he exited the Bentley and escorted him through the gates to the door in the middle of the famous black brick façade. Underneath the black paint the bricks were actually yellow. They were originally blackened by decades of exposure to the sooty London air, but when the façade was cleaned in the 1960's the public could not acclimate to the yellow, and they were re-blackened with paint.

Once they were through the door, the security officer led Wafiq to a comfortable, paneled sitting room hung with paintings depicting British politicians of the past and told him the Prime Minister would join him shortly.

He rose from the love seat in front of the marble fireplace when the door opened a few moments later and the Prime Minister came into the room. Her red hair perfectly coiffed, as usual, and wearing a black skirt with a double breasted matching top, she held out both hands to Wafiq and allowed him to brush his cheek against hers. The habitual pearls were around her neck, and Wafiq noted that her ears were adorned with diamonds.

The purpose of his visit was to resolve a particularly thorny matter involving financing for the *Al Sakir* arms sale – the Saudis were cash short and could not afford the large "good faith" payment required to seal the transaction. Once they had both sat down, Wafiq began, "I have heard from Riyadh, Prime Minister, and I fear the news I bring is not good."

"Oh dear," she responded, "So they really can't come up with the money?" He shook his head.

She skewered him with a penetrating gaze and held his eyes. She was well aware of the fact that the Saudis were facing a serious liquidity crisis. "But Prince Sultan assured us that his Government would be able to make at least the initial payment in cash."

This was a highly complex situation. With oil prices down, the Saudis were in no position to pay for anything in cash, let alone a multi-billion dollar arms purchase. For this reason, the Brits had agreed to the barter arrangement while the French dithered. The Saudis would give Shell and British Petroleum 300,000 barrels per day as payment with the proceeds going to Her Majesty's Government, but with oil prices down, even this would not cover the entire cost of the deal.

"The whole damned thing could fall apart on this issue, Wafiq," said the Prime Minister. Her voice acquired an edge.

Wafiq did not believe she would allow the arms sale which would revive the sagging British defense industry to fall through. Even if desperate measures were required, she was never one to shrink from a challenge. Moreover, British Aerospace had started production of the Tornado aircraft months ago and already begun to train Saudi flight crews. *Al Sakir* was a government-to-government agreement, and it was HMG that was to pay BAE from the proceeds of the oil sales, but some up-front "good will" cash still was required. Now the Saudi's had fallen short. Would she find a way out?

"Wafiq," she said, never dropping her steady gaze

from his face, "you of all people are aware of the importance of this matter. I want you to transmit to Prince Sultan that I will order HMG to provide one and a half billion pounds in loan guarantees to save the deal."

The British Embassy in Riyadh, of course, would have informed her of the Saudi liquidity crisis. Wafiq assumed she had anticipated this problem and already made the arrangements, which would have meant overcoming fierce resistance from Treasury and Bank of England officials.

He reminded himself never to underestimate this woman. He had not expected to leave this meeting with *Al Sakir* still intact.

"Prime Minister, you know what a risk you are taking?"

He was as anxious as anyone for the deal to go through because as its broker he would earn enormous commissions behind the scenes, commissions some might consider illegal but which were nonetheless the accepted way of doing business with Riyadh. Despite this, he still felt a duty to his friend, the Prime Minister, to urge some caution. He was, after all, a wealthy man already.

"Of course I do," she snapped back. It wasn't something she would have preferred. "You know that your friends in Riyadh outright refused to borrow funds so they could pay the up-front money themselves. This is the only way we can keep the thing moving forward. Now your task is to see to it that the Saudis do their part. Among other things, I must insist that they raise the daily oil quota to 400,000 barrels. And they'd damn well better make certain they deliver." She paused for effect, and then looked hard into Wafiq's eyes, "And not a word of this can leak. The consequences would be devastating for all concerned."

The Prime Minister, he knew, did not plan to disclose these controversial details to Parliament, just as she would not disclose the extraordinary accounting arrangements the deal required. She had classified this information as Official Secrets. She had also intervened with Government authorities to prevent the downgrading of Saudi Arabia's credit rating. She was gambling over a billion pounds of HMG's money that the Saudis would not default and back out of the deal at the last minute. She might wonder how much of the cash from the arms sales eventually would end up in private Saudi pockets. But this was an inevitability she had accepted from the start and in its own way it provided a strong incentive for the Saudis to go through with it all. Wafiq al Salah himself was likely eventually to realize a small fortune, but he was an ally and her direct private link to Prince Sultan, the Saudi Defense Minister. He was worth the price.

Wafiq left Nr. 10 Downing Street feeling weighed down by this information. *I've got to talk to Mohammed,* he thought, and used the car phone to set up a meeting that same afternoon.

Chapter 11

Walking through the Plexiglas tubes that made the interior of Charles DeGaulle Terminal 3 feel like a huge, futuristic ant colony, I experienced a dread not entirely unlike my recent arrival at Sheremetyevo. A dark, lowering sky provided an appropriate welcome. The French might well be waiting to snatch me and send me to the Château d'If, like the Count of Montecristo.

They wouldn't, but I was certain they'd like to.

Fortunately, the only person waiting for me was Kate. And she was the person I most wanted to see. I leaned back in the passenger seat of our Saab and closed my eyes for the long, tedious drive into Paris.

The United flight to Paris left Dulles in the afternoon and arrived in Paris around 7:00 AM, so I had grabbed a few hours' sleep on the way with the assistance of two double scotches. But I was knackered after spending a large portion of the preceding several days in the air. Gravity grabbed me like it does astronauts when they return from space and pressed me deeply into the seat. It was raining, and the sound of the water under the tires and splattering on the windshield would lull me to sleep if I didn't make an effort. The industrial landscape between Charles DeGaulle and the city wasn't much to look at anyway.

Kate, of course, wanted to talk.

"So tell me all about it." After a couple of weeks my recently brush-cut hair was growing out in messy, uncontrollable points, and she gave it a riffle with her free hand. "This isn't your new look, is it? I don't like it."

"You prefer running your fingers through my long, luxuriant tresses, do you? Does it turn you on?"

She smacked me up the side of the head.

"Ouch."

"No. We'll have to wait a month or so until it grows out for you to turn me on."

I assumed she was kidding. I hoped she was kidding.

"Terry called early this morning. He said he wants you in the office as soon as possible this morning."

"I'm not going straight to the office. We're going home where you can give me a proper welcome, and I'm going to take a shower and get some fresh duds. It feels like I've been wearing the same clothes for too long."

She flashed a wicked smile. "'A proper welcome,' huh. I suggest the shower come first."

And so it was, with a second shower *a dieux* as a bonus. I didn't make it to the Embassy until early afternoon.

Eileen gave me a frosty smile when I entered the front office suite. "We've been waiting for you."

"Domestic responsibilities come first, Eileen."

"Domestic responsibilities?"

I gave her my best leer. "That's right. And I always live up to my responsibilities."

"That's not exactly what I've been hearing," She smirked and waved toward Terry Stoddard's office door. "Go on in. But wipe the silly grin off your face."

"Yes, ma'am."

Terry greeted me with a weary smile. "I was afraid you might not show up, at all. You've been making up a lot of your own rules lately."

"All for the good of the home team," I said.

He stood and walked around his desk. "Have a seat," he said, heading for the leather sofa by the fireplace and waved a hand for me to follow.

Eileen came in carrying two steaming cups of coffee on a tray that she sat on the low table in front of the sofa. "I thought you might need some energy." She gave me a saucy glance over her shoulder on the way out of the office.

"I'm glad you survived the trip back to Headquarters," said Terry as he took a tentative sip of the hot coffee. "That was the kind of thing that can get a guy banished forever." He looked tired.

A week had passed since I'd skipped out on the DST.

"After they got a peek at what was on the film, Barton and Jerry Markham smoothed things over with the White House with some heavy lifting from the DCI himself."

Apparently the Barsikov files terrified everybody in Washington who saw them. Jerry Markham and the DCI personally briefed the President and Vice President, including my dalliance with independent thought. Happily for me, a jovial President told the DCI that he should give me a medal. Barton Graham decided that allowing me to keep my skin intact was reward enough. That was OK by me. I would have been a lousy short-order cook.

"It's not been a picnic here in Paris," said Terry. "The DST threatened to go to the Elysee and ask Mitterand to kick us all out. They were in high dudgeon when they figured out that you had skipped town with the goods."

"How did they find out?"

"It didn't take them long after you didn't show up to brief them on Moscow. It was my unhappy duty to confirm their suspicions under Headquarters instructions. I would have preferred to say nothing, but the order came from the Seventh Floor."

"Shit. Sorry about that, Terry. I guess being COS isn't always fun."

"Don't worry about it. Hell, I agreed with your plan. We did it together." Terry had agreed with my logic and authorized me to take the film directly to Langley. I would never have gone against Terry. He could have ordered me to turn the films over to the French. But he didn't. It meant putting his neck on the chopping block along with mine, and I appreciated it.

"We did the right thing, Terry."

He nodded. "I hope so. Fortunately for us both, oil has been poured over the waters. The President called Mitterand, and they reached an understanding."

"I'll bet they did."

"The DST had no choice but to accept the situation, but the agreement comes with a price."

"Let me guess. *Al Sakir.*"

The DST was a counter-intelligence outfit that did not possess the analytical capabilities of the CIA, and Terry Stoddard somehow convinced them it was a good idea for us to have the first look. Actually, it was. We promised to share with them things like the identities of KGB agents and undercover officers in France. This was the kind of stuff that counter-intelligence services live for. But what served to ease tensions the most was what Barsikov revealed about *Al Sakir*. Nothing warms the French soul more than a chance to poke a sharp dagger through British ribs.

Chapter 12

London

If anyplace in London can be called "posh," the Ritz Hotel heads the list. It was and still is the place to be seen. "Tea at the Ritz" has been a high privilege since the hotel opened in 1906.

While Wafiq al Salah was meeting with the Prime Minister, his old friend Mohammed Attar was meeting with another Brit, an easily corruptible one, over breakfast at the venerable hotel in Piccadilly at a discreet corner table in the ostentatiously decorated Palm Court room.

The mirrored walls, the fountain with is frolicking gilded statues, all brought to Mohammed's mind the image of a French whorehouse. How appropriate that he should be breakfasting there with a British whore.

James Abbott was the British Minister of State for Defense Procurement and, as such, was smack in the middle of *Al Sakir*. Born into the family of a Conservative Member of Parliament, in his time he had been a Tory backbencher himself. Despite a tincture of scandal that had blotted his political career at times, the roughly handsome, upper crust Abbott somehow retained the trust of his Tory government colleagues who had astonishingly appointed him Minister of State for Defense Procurement. This position put him in charge of negotiating foreign arms sales for HMG. When *Al Sakir* came along, Abbott was quick to recognize a once in a lifetime opportunity for self-enrichment and became one of the strongest proponents of the sale.

Abbott first met Attar at one of Prince's elaborate parties. The Brit was well aware of Attar's role as the Prince's principal assistant. He was also aware of the Prince's cupidity and at once concluded that there could be a meeting of the minds. There was no reason, he had boldly suggested to Attar, that the two could not work together for mutual profit. Attar readily agreed, and a crafty partnership was born. Both were determined to keep the mammoth arms deal on track no matter the costs.

Abbott provided the details and descriptions of the proposed weapons systems, and Attar, acting as the Prince's representative, explained to British weapons manufacturers that nothing is done with Saudi Arabia unless vendors are willing to pay "commissions." Over the months since the deal had been crafted various British companies had agreed to pay Attar "commissions" ranging from three to fifteen percent of the sales price. Attar, in turn, assured them that the Prince would guarantee that the prices they quoted would be accepted.

Besides aircraft and peripherals, they reached agreements on submarine sales, heavy self-propelled howitzers, and dozens of other weapons systems, among them some of Britain's most advanced. Attar and Abbott estimated that upwards of two hundred million dollars in kickbacks would flow into the Prince's coffers, with a sizeable chunk of that being diverted to their own pockets. Attar arranged several secret meetings for Abbott with Saudi arms experts. These meetings usually took place at the prestigious Ritz Hotel in Paris far away from London's prying eyes.

Now at the Palm Court Abbott was enthusiastically tucking into a full English breakfast while Mohammed picked disinterestedly at some melon slices. The British Minister, wearing a broadly pinstriped English suit and club tie, his boyish shock of brown hair falling across his forehead, was attentive to Mohammed's words.

"Unless HMG somehow comes through with loan guarantees, the deal is in danger of falling apart. The Prince is very upset, but even he can't control oil prices."

Mohammed Attar had come a long way from the insecurities of his youth. In fact, he had changed in ways even his best friends would never have suspected. People would now describe him as "austere" and "self-controlled," or "inscrutable." Despite his diminutive stature, he made his presence felt. He had adopted elegant, if conservative Western dress, perhaps more Continental in taste than British, and was always well turned out. His full head of black hair showed no sign of gray, and his short, expertly trimmed beard lent maturity and gravity to his face. His manner was self-assured. His Eddie Cantor eyes were now opaque rather than pleading. He had never married, a fact that his friend, Wafiq al Salah, mourned because he thought Mohammed was missing one of the greatest joys in life. He couldn't know that Mohammed had another sort of mistress.

Abbott abruptly put down his knife and fork and

wiped his mouth with a crisp, white napkin, a shocked expression on his face. He blurted, "My God, surely something can be done. Don't tell me The Kingdom is actually out of money!"

He was genuinely alarmed. The bribe money would not begin flowing in earnest until all the financing was in place.

"No liquid funds to spare at this time," said Mohammed. "My friend is meeting with the PM this morning, and I'll have a better idea of what's going on later today."

Wafiq kept Mohammed well informed of government-to-government progress on the deal. The two were working in tandem – Wafiq handled the higher-ups and Mohammed took care of the nitty-gritty details.

"But we've come so far," said Abbott, a whine creeping into his voice.

"Don't worry," soothed Mohammed, "all the players are already too deeply into the deal for it to fail. No one wants this to happen or needs it more than you Brits."

"I know, but I've taken some awful risks here. I deserve to be rewarded, and you know it. No matter what happens now."

Abbott could be a petulant child at times.

"James, my friend," said Mohammed quietly as he gripped Abbott's elbow. "You needn't worry so much. Besides, you know that when you leave Government, I will arrange a very well-paying job for you running one of the Prince's enterprises, regardless what might happen with *Al Sakir*. You are a friend."

In fact, it repelled Mohammed even to touch this

disgusting slug.

Only slightly mollified, Abbott found he had lost his appetite and pushed his half-empty plate away. Reaching under the table for his briefcase, he said, "I have some new documents for you to show the Prince."

He extracted a large envelope with the HMG seal in the corner. "These are from Westland - specifications for a new model of the Blackhawk helicopter the Saudi's want."

Mohammed quickly scanned the room. No one was looking in their direction. *The Brits are great ones for minding their own business,* he thought. He took the envelope and placed it underneath his raincoat on the chair next to his.

"Thank you, James. These will be very helpful."

In fact, just as all the other weapons specifications Abbott had passed to him over the past several months, these would eventually find their way to more interested hands. The Prince didn't care a fig about such documents and had never seen a single one. Mohammed would, of course, pass them to the Russians, but not before making copies for a Saudi eye surgeon who lived in north London and communicated regularly with the Sheik.

Chapter 13

Rule No. 1

No. 2 *Place des Saussaies* had not changed since my last visit. The steady drumbeat of the rain on my umbrella punctuated my mood. It had been falling steadily since my arrival that morning.

I walked from the Embassy anyway. It was a way of delaying the inevitable confrontation with my old friend, Jacques Picard. The rain infused the air with its fresh scent and cleansed the streets, but it would not wash away my sins.

After a twenty-minute very damp trudge I halted on the wet cobblestones in front of the entrance. It consisted of double doors of heavy wood, for some reason painted sky blue. There was an ancient looking brass handle in the middle of the right door that looked more like a ring pull. According to a plaque beside the door, the composer Francois Poulenc had been born there in 1839. I was sure he never could have imagined the uses to which his birthplace would be put.

Terry Stoddard and I had concluded our *tete-à-tete* at around two o'clock. We decided it would be best if I faced the music alone. It wasn't that Terry was a coward. He was the Chief of Station, Paris, a rather exalted position, and I insisted it would not be right for him to endure any French opprobrium, if that's what the frogs had in mind.

Terry didn't protest too much.

The rain intensified, splashing over my shoes, and I twisted the brass handle and shoved it open.

I'd been debating how to approach the meeting

with Picard. A cynical and unapologetic approach was tempting and mirrored the way a French official would have handled it. They can be nervelessly disdainful when they choose. *(Qu'est que vous pensez? C'est un rien.)* But I discarded mimicry in favor of a shamelessly honest approach. I thought it might confuse the French.

My formerly benign opinion of Lafayette's people had changed, if only temporarily. But if I wanted to be completely honest, they had a right to be upset, and to tell the truth I almost felt guilty.

Almost.

The guard waved me through to the same stone walled room as last time.

Picard wasn't there. Instead, his assistant, Dominique Thibault was behind the desk smoking a Gauloise Blonde. François Mitterrand's eyes followed my movements from the photo on the wall. He looked hostile today.

Thibault was somewhere in his mid-30's, a tall, handsome dishwater blond with a trim figure that he carried with a languorous nonchalance that would have looked good on a fashion show runway. He stood when I entered and gave me a crooked smile and hung my dripping coat and umbrella on a coat rack that stood beside the door.

"Jacques will be along shortly," he said. "Have a seat." He waved languidly in the direction of a chair.

Picard had decided to make me wait, a small penance.

"You've been travelling a lot of late," observed Thibault.

I ignored the observation. I wasn't about to be

interrogated by one of Picard's subordinates.

I asked, "How long will he be?"

He shrugged. "I'm not sure. He's in a meeting."

"He has a meeting with me."

"Well, he's been trying to see you for several days now, hasn't he? But he had to wait."

Jeez, they weren't even being subtle.

"All the more reason for him to want to see me now."

Thibault smiled. "He knows you're here. I'm sure he'll be along shortly. He's with the Director. Would you like some coffee?"

A gesture of hospitality or a hint that I would have to wait a good while before Picard joined us?

"Sure, why not?"

Thibault made a short phone call, and a few minutes later a young woman came in bearing a small tray with two white cups of espresso nestling on saucers and a bowl of sugar cubes.

I sniffed the coffee carefully, testing for arsenic. I downed it in a single gulp. I really like French coffee.

Thibault replaced his cup in its saucer and lit another Gauloise. "You look tired, Harry."

I was tired despite the coffee with Terry and the cup I'd just swallowed. I didn't feel like making small talk with Thibault. The wooden chair was damned uncomfortable.

At that moment, the door in the wall behind me, the door that communicated with the interior of DST Headquarters, opened.

Jacques Picard strode into the room. I stood and extended my hand, which he regarded for a beat before taking. I couldn't read the expression on his face.

Nobody was smiling.

Thibault surrendered his seat behind the desk to his superior and took a chair beside me.

Picard clasped his hands together on the desktop. "Welcome back to Paris, Harry. We thought we might have lost you."

I wasn't sure how to respond. "I've been busy," I said.

"You certainly have. Lucien Gagnon told us the meeting in Moscow had not been a success. You can imagine our surprise when your Chief of Station informed us otherwise."

"Lucien Gagnon, nice guy that he is, is a trade representative. He doesn't need to know anything more than he already does."

"That's really something for us to decide," said a still unsmiling Picard. "He is our confidential informant, and he had a role to play in the Moscow affair."

"And he played his part perfectly. There was no need for further involvement."

Picard cocked his head to one side and made that sound of disappointment and disgust so popular with the French. *"Pah."* It's not a loud sound, but rather a soft explosion of breath from the front of the mouth through slightly parted lips. They usually accompany it with a shake of the head and half-closed eyes; as though they had decided there was no hope for you.

They weren't going to let the thing pass without expressing their annoyance. Maybe it was because I was exhausted that I said, "Look, Jacques, you know as well as anyone that there are only two rules in espionage: Rule No. 1 – There are friendly countries, but there are no friendly intelligence services; Rule No. 2 – There are no other rules."

Harsh, but true. Maybe there is more cynicism than trust in intelligence work, after all.

"We were, we are, very disappointed, Harry." There was annoyance in his eyes now. "After all, we did share our operation with you." He emphasized the word "our."

I decided to try using logic. The French are very fond of Descartes and logic.

"Yes, and for good reason. This should be a terrific operation. But one of the things the volunteer told us without being too specific was that he was aware of KGB spies in France, as well as the UK. It was not the best idea to turn all of that film over to you before we knew who the spies were. It could even have been Gagnon."

His annoyance was replaced by indignation, but it got his attention. "Are you saying there is a Russian mole in the DST? Do you think I'm a mole?"

"It wouldn't make any sense if you were the mole. We don't have the list yet. They're still working on the film at Langley."

"So, it was on the grounds of baseless speculation that you took our intelligence?"

"Jacques, you know that the only reason the CIA became involved at all was the strong likelihood that the bulk of information coming from Directorate 'T' would concern the theft of American technology. That was your hook. You set it deep, and it worked. I think we both should look at this as a successful operation. Your interests are high on Langley's priority list. We've already begun processing the information, and there is a hell of a lot of it. Anything that concerns France will be passed to you immediately. It should keep you quite busy."

It would take months to process and analyze all of the Barsikov documents. Even more difficult would be deciding how to use the information. Obviously, compromised weapons systems would have to be scrapped or modified. The lists of VPK requirements included with the documents might well tell us everything we needed to know about Soviet technological shortcomings.

Picard still looked pretty cranky. Thibault was staying out of it.

Langley had authorized Terry and me to offer something that might smooth the DST's ruffled feathers.

"We still consider this a joint operation," I began in my best earnest voice. "We intend to work it together with you as equals. From the documents we've seen so far it's pretty clear that we have information concerning several other allied countries. We thought it would be a good idea if such information were to be disseminated by France. We're not interested in taking any of the credit, and we'll be busy patching up the holes we find in our own back fence."

Picard perked up a little. His chances of being awarded the *Legión d'Honneur* may have brightened.

"You're saying that ALL information disseminated to allies will be handled by us?"

"Well ... When the time is right, so long as we can protect the source."

"Including the Brits?"

This was ticklish. The Brits are our closest allies,

one of "The Five Eyes" alliance: the US, the UK, Canada, Australia, and New Zealand. There isn't much that isn't shared aside from purely operational details.

Picard wasn't backing down. "Specifically *Al Sakir*? It will be our decision?"

We'd figured this was coming.

"On one condition - the KGB operation must be compromised."

Chapter 14

London

Becky heard the crunch of gravel in the circular front drive as she descended the main staircase still fastening her earrings. Through a window she saw Mohammed Attar's familiar old Mercedes pulling to a stop under the front portico. *When will he ever trade that old wreck in on a new car? He can certainly afford it.*

She wasn't especially fond of Mohammed. She found him stand-offish and not a little disapproving in his manner. She chalked this up to Arab cultural attitudes toward women in general, attitudes her husband had managed to overcome and eschew, thank God. Regardless, the mysterious little man was her husband's friend of many years. There was a deep bond between these men, and Becky was a wise enough woman to know it would be a mistake to get between them.

She opened the door and stepped outside to greet him as the diminutive Lebanese mounted the steps, "Mohammed! So good to see you again. Please, come in." He wore gray slacks, a blue blazer, and a silk crew neck sweater.

Attar paused for a moment on the threshold, for the hundredth time appraising the petite, doll-like blonde Englishwoman who had somehow captivated his friend. He involuntarily recalled his initial disappointment when he had learned of Wafiq's marriage to an infidel. It had been difficult to control his resentment of her. Wafiq had become entirely too westernized, but Mohammed could never overcome his affection for his best friend.

Becky took his arm, and he suppressed a slight shudder at the familiarity of the touch.

"It's good to see you, too, Becky," he said in the polite voice he reserved for these occasions. Becky was sufficiently familiar with him by now to know better than to attempt a peck on the cheek.

She led him to the sitting room where the maid had earlier set out a tray with an assortment of fruit juices and invited Mohammed to sit.

"Wafiq will be down in a moment," she said. "He had a busy day today. I gather the meeting with the Prime Minister went well."

"We'll see," said Mohammed. He definitely did not believe in discussing business with women. He wondered how Wafiq put up with it.

Becky turned with a grateful look at the sound of her husband hurrying down the stairs. He had changed to informal dress – dark green corduroys and a white cotton pull-over.

The two men greeted one another with an embrace and a kiss on each cheek.

"Salaam Aleikhem," the traditional greeting and reverse response.

"Sit down, Mohammed, sit down," invited Wafiq. What can I fix you to drink?"

"Orange juice will be fine," said Mohammed.

Becky was already missing the evening cocktail she and her husband normally imbibed. Unlike Wafiq, Mohammed strictly avoided alcohol. So, tonight, once again, Wafiq would play the pious Muslim for his friend's sake. Becky planned to mix herself a gin and tonic as soon as she was inevitably dismissed by the men. She would be glad to leave them to their business.

Later, as the maid was clearing the remains of dinner from the table, Wafiq gave her a look that meant it's time for the men to talk.

"Well," she said, rising to excuse herself, "I can see that you men have important matters to discuss that would bore me to death. Would you excuse me, Mohammed? I think I'll go upstairs and read."

Mohammed rose and bowed slightly, "Of course, Becky. Thank you for a very fine meal. Your hospitality is perfect, as usual."

After she had disappeared upstairs, Wafiq led Mohammed to the study. The room was self-consciously English with its rich wood paneling, brass lamps, and leather wing chairs. It could have been a room at one of the private clubs on Pall Mall. It smelled of leather, books, and tobacco. The fully stocked bar was concealed in a bookcase.

Wafiq offered his friend a cigarette from a multi-colored enameled box. Mohammed accepted. Wafiq had them custom made by Dunhill using a particular mixture of tobaccos he had chosen.

Wafiq took a silver lighter from a side table and handed it to his friend. Mohammed appreciated its heft. He lit up and passed it back. Wafiq selected a short, thick cigar from a walnut humidor.

The two sat facing one another in the high backed chairs in front of the fireplace.

"How did it go with the Prime Minister today?" asked Mohammed.

As usual when the two were alone they switched

to Arabic.

Wafiq frowned slightly at the memory of the conversation. "She's taking some big risks and keeping the details to herself," he finally said. "Our friends in Riyadh are a bit skittish. The price of oil is squeezing them these days."

Mohammed nodded. "James Abbott is certainly worried, but that's not a bad thing. It keeps him on his toes dancing to our tune."

Wafiq's lips curled slightly at the mention of the distasteful Abbott – just another cog in a wheel that required a lot of grease. "The Prime Minister will keep things on track on the British side, but can we count on the Prince to maintain forward momentum in Riyadh?"

"The Prince will do whatever I tell him. He has too much riding on this horse to let it fail. I think we will have to set up a meeting of principals to seal the matter. It will take a couple of weeks, but we can use the Prince's villa in Geneva. Can you line up the Brits?"

"The British need this deal badly, very badly, and the Prime Minister is willing to go to almost any length to preserve it, even to the point of risking her position."

Mohammed took a pull from his cigarette and nodded somberly.

Wafiq was not for the first time struck by the transformation of Mohammed from the naïve, carefree youngster he had befriended so many years ago to the serious player in international intrigue that sat before him now.

Chapter 15

Warsaw, Poland - 1974

Seated together in the Air France first class cabin, the two young men scanned the city tilting under the wingtip of the plane as it circled for a landing at Warsaw's Okięcia International Airport.

While Wafiq was tall and handsome, with olive skin and thick black curls, Mohammed was slight. His skin was pale, and his eyes were quite round and large, lending him a look of perpetual surprise.

The two had booked a luxury suite at the new Forum Hotel in the city center, and they alighted from the airport cab like princes of the world, tossing dollars right and left to a delighted hotel staff that treasured hard currency like prospectors panning for gold nuggets. They knew a rich stream when they saw one. The hotel, a western style glass tower, had been constructed by a Swedish firm for Orbis, the Polish state tourist organization, and was one of the few skyscrapers in all of post-war Poland, apart from the Stalinesque Palace of Culture just a few blocks away.

Warsaw in 1974 was a drab Eastern European capital tinted in tones of gray and dirty yellow. All the bright color had been sucked out by war and a ruthless Communist regime. Polish winters were cold and nasty, and the fallen snow was covered overnight with a layer of black grime from the Silesian coal that heated the city and ran its factories. But Warsaw did hold a certain distinction, a sort of salacious infamy among its sister Soviet Bloc capitals. The Poles were a cosmopolitan race and their ancient capital was well-known for a lifestyle looser than that normally found in the totalitarian Eastern Bloc. There were even strippers who entertained the commissars in the basement nightclub of the venerable *Hotel Europejski* on *Krakowskie Przedmieście*, a broad thoroughfare that ran from the city center up to the Old Town Square.

Occasionally the city attracted exotic guests curious to see what life was like in a Communist state and well aware that the hard currency they brought with them was highly sought after in the workers' paradise. Fleshly pleasures were easily accessible for foreigners with the right kind of money.

In 1974 Mohammed Attar was 25 years old and foolish, as young men everywhere tend to be. His father was Lebanese, but his mother was from a well-connected Saudi family distantly related to the Saudi royals. From an early age his mother had seen to it that he spent a great deal of time in The Kingdom as Lebanon became increasingly dangerous. His mother also had ensured that he was accepted by Saudis his own age from much wealthier families, and he came to appreciate the privileges wealth can bestow. His young Saudi friends were faultlessly generous.

Of his many Saudi friends, the closest to Mohammed was Wafiq al Salah, two years older than Mohammed, and a cousin of King Fahd. In the winter of 1974 while on holiday in Europe the two decided on a whim to visit Warsaw. Their enthusiasm for the trip was infused with fantasies they concocted about the lusty blond girls they would find there and what they would do with them.

They had seen enough of the world to know that once away from the restrictions of Riyadh they were free to discard religious inhibitions and indulge in every "infidel" vice they could imagine, so long as their money held out – and there was no possibility that Wafiq al Salah would ever run out of money.

The two spent their first day exploring the city and returned to the hotel quite disappointed with the poor quality of the goods they had seen in the shops and the scarcity of restaurants. They were appalled by the Poles' national affinity for pork products and considered themselves fortunate to have found a small restaurant in the *Stare Miasto,* Old Town area that specialized in roast duck.

In their suite on the 14th floor, Wafiq flopped heavily onto the sofa. "This place is a hole! Let's get out of here as soon as we can."

"I agree," said Mohammed. "This whole trip was a big mistake. Whose idea was it to leave Paris for a week-end and come here anyway? Pretty stupid."

Wafiq's eyes crinkled with his easy smile, his perfect white teeth broadly on display. "You idiot," he said fondly, "You know whose idea it was – yours!"

"I know, I know," laughed the young Lebanese. "But do you know what? We can't leave this place until we've bagged a couple of blondes. What do you say?"

"What do you think I say? And you know what? We don't have to look very far. I was talking to the bartender downstairs earlier today. There are girls, professional girls, available right here in the hotel. I think we should go downstairs, have the bartender hook us up, treat the girls to a great dinner and bring them back up here. We have a night of fun and get the hell out on the first flight back to Paris."

"That is an excellent plan, my brother," said

Mohammed, his eyes shining. Wafiq was a good man, a good friend, and was always kind to the diminutive Mohammed. Mohammed truly loved him as a brother.

Wafiq's plan was put to the test, and the two young men soon found themselves enjoying a meal in the Forum's ostentatious main restaurant with two ladies who said their names were Wanda and Danuta. Mohammed was slightly disappointed that Danuta, his girl, was a brunette, but she was petite and very well shaped. Handsome Wafiq, of course, ended up with the buxom blonde, Wanda.

They finished the meal, an enthusiastically served but disappointingly bland affair, with a chilled bottle of Russian *shampanskoye* that Wafiq found pleasantly sweet. Silence descended over the table as the inexperienced young men suddenly discovered that they didn't know quite what to say next.

Wanda solved the problem for them. She wasn't about to let these rich boys get away. "Why don't you order more *shampanskoye* up to your room, and we can all go up and have a party?"

Mohammed and Wafiq thought this was a great idea. They pushed back from the table and the girls clung tightly to them, smiling like a couple of kids on Christmas morning. Danuta coyly suggested that they make a stop at the dollar store in the hotel's main lobby. "They have French bras and panties this week. Do you think we would look good in such things? We could give you a fashion show."

The boys didn't hesitate for a second. Wafiq caught Mohammed's eyes and said in Arabic, "Didn't I tell you this was a great idea?"

They loaded the delighted prostitutes down with

French lingerie, French perfume, and new handbags, and the jolly crew headed for the elevators closely followed by a uniformed bellhop pushing a serving cart laden with pastries, two iced bottles of *shampanskoye*, and a bottle of Johnny Walker Black Label.

The girls oohed and ahhed at the sight of the luxurious 14th floor suite. When they saw the spacious bathroom with oversized tub, they insisted on a bath and began stripping off their clothes as Wafiq and Mohammed stood at the bathroom door with stupid grins creasing their faces.

There was a lot of splashing and giggling, and the boys were nearly rapturous at the sight of Danuta and Wanda both in the large tub, their bodies covered with suds. Apparently hot water in abundance was something of a luxury in Poland.

Wanda, the blond, was statuesque, and when she stood in the tub it was clear that she was a natural blond. Wafiq was mesmerized and swayed for a moment as though he might faint.

Danuta was petite where Wanda was generously proportioned, but regarding her as she stood dripping on the bathroom floor, Mohammed suddenly decided he didn't care anymore that she wasn't a blonde.

An hour later, the boys' jack-o' lantern grins now transformed to satisfied smiles, the four re-grouped in the main room of the suite and started on the first bottle of shampanskoye, most of the ice in the buckets having by now melted. The girls decided to put on their new lingerie and try out the perfume from the dollar shop. Wafiq found what passed for a rock station on the radio, and the Russian bubbly soon disappeared.

This was definitely the best 'party' Wanda and Danuta had ever had. By two in the morning, the scotch had all but disappeared and all of them were finding it hard to stand without a bit of weaving. The music was still playing, and Danuta turned up the volume insisting she wanted to dance.

She stood in front of Mohammed and swayed her body seductively as she reached behind her back and unhooked her new bra. She let it fall to the floor and bent down to him, rubbing her breasts against his face. "*Yes*", thought Mohammed, his eyes closed with pleasure, "*this is what it's all about! I could die happy right now.*"

He rose to take Danuta in his arms and they began whirling to the music, the alcohol in their systems making them giddy.

Afterwards, Mohammed could not recall precisely how it happened, but Danuta suddenly spun out of his grasp. One moment she was there, and the next she was gone.

Seriously tipsy and off balance, she teetered over and smashed full force into the window. Had the hotel been built strictly to Western standards, she would have bounced back into the room onto the floor, still drunk, but only dazed. Unfortunately, the Swedish contractors had cut some corners by bribing the Polish officials in charge of building inspection. The below-standard glass window shattered under the impact of the girl's body, and she hurtled, screaming, out into the cold Warsaw night, plunging 14 stories to a messy death below on the sidewalk beside Ulica Marszalkowska, one of the city's main drags.

Mohammed, Wafiq, and Wanda gaped in stunned disbelief. For a second no one spoke, and then Wanda screamed. Her face contorted with loathing and fear, she was looking right at Mohammed, "What happened? What did you do?!!!"

Horrified, Mohammed turned toward them, his arms spread helplessly as the cold, polluted air of Warsaw's winter filled the room through the shattered window. "I don't know what happened! I don't know!"

Even in her inebriated state Wanda knew this was real trouble that would carry dire consequences. She began gathering her things, frantic to get out of the room. Using one of the oversize bathrobes from the bathroom as a makeshift carry all, she wrapped everything, including Danuta's clothes and gifts, and jerked on her dress. She ran out the door and disappeared, still wailing as she ran down the hall.

Wafiq turned off the music, and the two young men sat together on the sofa in stunned silence until the pulsating scream of a klaxon cut through the night, growing louder each second like a banshee on its way to collect their souls.

After what seemed an eternity, there was a loud banging on the door of the suite, and before they could rise from the sofa, it burst open to reveal three police officers in gray uniforms with their side arms drawn. A grim visaged man in civilian clothing followed them into the room.

Chapter 16

When Danuta Novikova hurtled 14 stories to a messy death there were few people out in the pre-dawn morning to witness the event. The hotel doorman rushed into the street and looked up the brightly illuminated side of the building to see the shattered window on the 14th floor.

Hotel staff immediately divined the source of the trouble. The *młodzi Arabowie,* young Arabs. When the excited doorman rushed into the lobby to report what had happened, the manager called the hotel security chief, who in turn reported the incident to the *Milicja.*

Within moments two green and white Militia cars screeched to a halt at the hotel's main entrance, klaxons blaring, followed by an unmarked car. All were *Polski* Fiat 125p's, of Polish manufacture.

Captain Jerzy Kowałczyk of the Polish security service, the *Służba Bezpieczeństwa,* exited the unmarked car and conferred with the group of uniformed officers gathered at the hotel entrance. He ordered two men to secure the impact site and cordon it off. Another he told to obtain witness statements. Satisfied that his instructions were being carried out, he entered the hotel with three of the uniforms.

Jan Kuczynski, the hotel security chief, was waiting just inside, breathless with excitement. Kowałczyk spotted a young, blond woman in a state of partial *déshabille* who was being questioned by one of Kuczynski's men in a far corner of the lobby. He jerked his head in her direction and raised an eyebrow at the security chief.

"A witness," said Kuczynski, "She saw what happened up there. It was only a matter of time until something like this happened with those Arab animals. I have a man upstairs guarding their door."

"Give me the names of the suspects, as well as their passports and any other documentation you have," Kowałczyk ordered.

"*Tak toczno, pan Kapitan.* Immediately!" Kuczynski rushed to the reception desk while Kowałczyk took three uniforms in the elevator to the 14th floor.

Upon entering the suite they discovered two young men huddled, shivering on the sofa wearing nothing but their boxer shorts despite the lowered temperature in the room. The taller of the two had his arm around a small, pale fellow with large, round eyes.

He rose on unsteady legs to address Kowałczyk. "My name is Wafiq Al-Salah. There has been an accident." He spoke in English.

Kowałczyk looked him up and down, his face expressionless. Ignoring the young foreigner's ridiculous statement, he said in the same language, "Sit back down and wait to be questioned about what happened in this room. I suggest that you answer truthfully."

Kowałczyk intended to examine the crime scene before questioning the suspects, but the boy wasn't backing down, and his next words grated on Kowałczyk's ears.

"My father is a cousin to King Fahd, and I carry a diplomatic passport. I demand you call the Royal

Saudi Embassy at once!"

The sound of Kowałczyk's open palm striking the side of the young man's face echoed off the walls. The boy was stunned.

"How dare you strike me, you pig," he shouted and then made another mistake by taking a threatening step toward the SB Captain. The three militia men charged forward, and Wafiq stared down in disbelief at three pistols pressed hard against his chest.

Kowałczyk's voice was icy. "Your country has no Embassy in Poland. It may take some time, possibly a long time, to contact any representative of your government, at all. In the meantime, we are dealing here with a capital crime, and I don't care what kind of passport you are carrying. You're not a diplomat in Poland."

The uniforms roughly shoved Wafiq back to the couch where he sat, but Kowałczyk could tell that he was still seething with the insult to his person.

His words dripping with disdain, Kowałczyk spoke slowly and clearly. "A Polish citizen, apparently a young girl was murdered here tonight. Do you really think your petrodollars exempt you from the law? This is a country ruled by Socialist justice, and I assure you that someone will pay for this murder. Someone will spend many years as a guest of our fine penal system."

He felt nothing but sour contempt for these *młodzi Arabowie*. "You animals should have stayed in the desert fucking camels."

Turning to the uniforms he instructed, "Get them dressed, cuff them and bring them to Headquarters."

He began his inspection of the crime scene, noting especially the empty bottles and glasses. It was plain to see what had happened here.

Chapter 17

Number 5, Ulica Stefana Batoriego

The two increasingly panicked young men were allowed to dress and then perp-walked across the wide expanse of the hotel lobby and outside where they were bundled into the back of one of the green and white Fiat patrol cars. With klaxons pulsating high-low notes the car tore south down Marszałkowska before veering right into a broad street called Puławska. Within five minutes of leaving the hotel the car screeched to a halt in the courtyard of an ominous stone building at Number 5, *Ulica Stefana Batoriego*. This was the Ministry of Interior, the ruling body of the Polish Republic's intelligence and internal security services. The two prisoners were escorted inside, none too gently, and through a maze of dimly lit corridors to a bare, gray room where they were instructed to sit on a hard wooden bench ranged against the far wall. A gray-uniformed, stone faced guard observed their entrance disinterestedly from behind a metal desk across the room.

Kowalczyk's chauffeured car arrived an hour later. He had thoroughly examined the crime scene at the hotel and retrieved the passports and other documents of the prisoners from the hotel security chief. The uniform he had assigned to find witnesses had come up empty handed. His brief on-the-spot interrogation of the prostitute, Wanda, had yielded the salient facts of the case. The slimy little Lebanese worm with the big puppy eyes was clearly guilty of manslaughter, if not murder. He would hang or spend many years in a Polish prison. Nobody cared about the Lebanese.

But the Saudi was another matter. His country hefted a lot of weight internationally, and the blood relationship to the Saudi King, if true, would guarantee some noise in the Western press. They undoubtedly would claim this was a frame-up, that any signed confession the Poles might produce had been coerced. The final decision on this case would be made at a much higher level, but for now Kowalczyk was in charge, and he would do a thorough job.

A guard confirmed that the prisoners were in the holding cell, and Kowalczyk headed down the hall to Interrogation Room Number 3 to prepare for what he expected would be a long day. It was already nearing another frigid dawn in the Polish capital. The SB Captain spread the prisoners' documents across the desk, arranging them in two groups. He took his time going through them.

It was nine A.M. before Wafiq and Mohammed were escorted from the holding cell to Interrogation Room No. 3, where Kowalczyk waited with humorless, black-rimmed eyes behind a desk. The ashtray beside his hand was filled with butts and the room reeked of cheap tobacco.

The walls were of bare, gray stone, the floor of cement, and Wafiq noticed that there was a large grated drain in the center of the floor from which a fetid odor rose. A bright light was shining directly into his eyes, and through a miasma of cigarette smoke that hung in motionless, blue layers, he could barely make out the SB officer seated behind the metal desk. The guard pushed him and Mohammed onto two wooden chairs facing the desk. At a gesture from Kowałczyk, the guard unlocked the cuffs and twisted their arms behind the backs of the chairs, where they were again locked. This was an uncomfortable position, and the wooden chair backs bit painfully into their arms.

Wafiq squinted, trying to get a better look at the Polish official. Every story he had ever heard about the terrors of Communist prisons reverberated in his mind. Kowałczyk still did not utter a word. He leaned back, chain lit another cigarette, and simply stared malevolently at the young men.

Kowałczyk noted that the Saudi was trying to get a better look at him, but the Lebanese hung his head, perhaps to avoid the bright light, perhaps to conceal his face and his guilt. This was a good sign. The Captain had interrogated hundreds of prisoners, some of them hard to break, some easy. These two would be easy, especially the slimy little Lebanese.

They sat in silence until Wafiq, impatient as usual, could stand it no longer.

"Well, what do you intend to do? You can't keep us here." He tried to sound angry, but his rising panic caused his voice to break.

Kowałczyk studied them for a moment longer and his expression turned to disgust, as if he were observing particularly repellant insects under a glass. His voice when he spoke dripped with sarcasm.

"Since you ask, here is what will happen, Mr. Salah. You will confess to the murder of Danuta

Nowikova, Polish citizen, 19 years old. You will do this in writing, and you will sign the confessions. You may write in Arabic, if you like. We have excellent linguists available. When you are ready to write, I will instruct the guard to free your hands. Or, if you prefer, we can compose the documents ourselves. All you have to do is sign."

He shoved two pads of yellow paper and two ball-point pens across the desk toward Wafiq and Mohammed and sat back. His chair squeaked as he rocked back and forth. "I will have your hands freed whenever you are ready to write."

Finally processing what the Polish officer had said, Wafiq croaked, "We didn't kill anybody! We never did! What happened was an accident." A thought occurred to him, "I will pay the girl's parents a handsome compensation for the loss of their daughter ... the TRAGIC loss of their daughter." The payment of so-called "blood money" was an old and honored tradition among Arabs.

Kowałczyk brought his fist down on the desk with such force that the pens and paper jumped into the air. He snarled the ancient Polish insult into the prisoners' faces, "*Psa krev*!! Dog's blood!! The Polish Republic is a socialist state ruled by socialist justice. The girl's parents have no need of your filthy money. They will be well taken care of by the state. Now, stop wasting my time. Shall I free your hands so you can write out a confession?"

Captain Kowałczyk explained in excruciating detail what would happen to them in the Polish penal system, assuring them that there was no hope if they refused to confess and then were convicted of murder.

"There is no doubt you will be convicted, by the way. The friend of the girl you murdered has given us all the testimony we require. You found two innocent young Polish girls on the street, enticed them to your room, debauched them, and in a drunken rage you," and here he pointed to Mohammed, "threw her through a plate glass window."

"But, Sir," said Wafiq struggling to achieve a reasonable tone, "they were prostitutes. Surely the people at the hotel will confirm that. And it was an accident. Mohammed did not push the girl through the window. She simply stumbled and fell into it. It was an accident," he repeated, desperation now constricting his throat and making his voice tiny. To make matters worse his head was pounding from the after effects of the alcohol he had consumed.

Kowalczyk stood, walked around the desk and struck the bound Wafiq with his fist, full in the face, smashing the Saudi's nose and knocking him, still bound to the chair, to the floor. A sudden gush of blood spilled over the front of his shirt. Mohammed helplessly witnessed the scene as his friend nearly passed out from the blow and the pain.

A guard rushed in to right Wafiq's chair. Kowalczyk bent low over him and screamed into his ear, "There are NO prostitutes in the Polish Republic! This is a socialist state and such capitalistic degradation of women is not permitted! You will not repeat such lies!"

The Captain knew perfectly well that Warsaw's population of prostitutes was numerous. In fact, such women were required to share their earnings with the state and were managed by SB agents under cover as bartenders, hoteliers, etc. who mined them for information on the foreigners they serviced. He simply hated the thought of them doing business with these dark skinned Arabs.

Chapter 18

I was spending so much time in the air between Paris and Washington that I was on a first-name basis with the United flight crews. They insured that I got a comfortable seat alone in the rear of the Business Class cabin and were extra generous with the single malt from First Class.

After we got our heads around the information on the films, Barton Graham invited me to lunch at the Army and Navy Club on Farragut Square. I was happy to escape the corridors of Headquarters where I kept bumping into people I knew but could not tell them why I was spending so much time there of late. Compartmentalization can be uncomfortable, especially when you're surrounded daily by smart spooks who can sniff out that something special is going on. They also were smart enough not to ask any questions.

Graham arranged for a company car with a driver, which was nice and spared us the walk from a parking garage to the Club in Washington's humid 90-degree summer.

I'm not a very clubby guy, but I've always admired this one. The venerable club is a vestige of a more elegant era and is filled with historic memorabilia, including the flag that was hoisted on Stephen Decatur's ship. The whole place is a study in American history. One of my favorite facts is that the first Daiquiri in the United States was consumed here, introduced in 1909 by Admiral Lucius W. Johnson. The drink was named after the beach on which the American Expeditionary Force landed in Cuba.

The wood paneled dining room is large with huge,

torch like sconces spaced evenly along the walls. It is dominated by a huge and excellent reproduction of the Landsdowne portrait of George Washington by Gilbert Stuart. We had no problem finding an isolated table by a window with a view of uncomfortable Washingtonians scurrying along outside in search of their next air-conditioned refuge.

Lunch with Graham was a rare event, and he'd given no particular reason for the invitation. I wondered if it might be some sort of atonement for his earlier behavior toward me.

But, of course, it wasn't.

He wasn't much for small-talk, and as soon as our plates were delivered he got right down to business.

"Harry, I want to talk to you about this Directorate 'T' business. You may already have realized its significance. The material from Moscow opens an entirely new vista on KGB operations on behalf of the Military Industrial Commission, the VPK. They have established a complex system of front companies and foreign bank accounts and are abetted by witting and venal agents in industry and trade. Thanks to Barsikov, we now have a fairly complete picture of their operation. Maybe even more important is what we've learned from their shopping list about Soviet weaknesses. The White House intends to use this information to wage all-out economic warfare against the USSR. The President means to take them down."

"So the plan is to deny them the technology they need to keep up with the West?"

"Defensive measures are part of it, of course, and I'll get to that in a minute, but there are other possibilities. We've been tasked with planning active measures, as well."

"Covert action?"

Graham levered a spoonful of Boston clam chowder to his mouth. "Yes."

Why was he telling me this?

The chowder was good, and we finished our bowls in silence. I figured Graham would say what he had to say when he was ready.

"We'll have to work in close coordination with the French on this. We owe them a great deal, and the White House is inclined to give them their due."

The CIA was normally stingy with its operations, but this was a special case, and Graham's words pleased me.

"I agree."

I had interrupted his narrative. "Magnanimous of you, Harry, to agree with a Headquarters decision for a change."

I wasn't about to try to match sarcasm for sarcasm with Graham. He was too good at it. I decided to wait him out and tucked into my main course.

He chewed on his steak for a few minutes before continuing. "Because the French will be intimately involved, Paris Station, and you specifically have a large role to play. We're keeping the operational aspects on a strict need-to-know basis. This means that we're going to put the operational as well as the liaison onus on you."

"What exactly does that mean?"

"It means you're going to tote up an enormous number of frequent flyer miles."

I thought I caught a rare twinkle in Graham's eyes. "And you have your decision to bring that material directly to Washington to thank for the assignment. Well done."

The prospects for long week-ends at Compiegne got a whole lot dimmer.

"The first problem we face is how to disseminate the information to our friends."

"We agreed to let the French handle that."

"Well, they'll handle some of it, but we've had some afterthoughts." He crammed a forkful of mashed potatoes into his mouth.

Crap. If we renege on the promise I'd made to Picard life would become even more difficult in Paris. I like Paris. I wanted to stay there as long as possible.

"We're not going to renege on them, are we?"

Graham's lips twitched in a tight smile as he wiped them with his napkin. "Aren't you listening? I just said we'll be working closely with them."

"Okay."

"I just think it's a bad idea for all the information sharing to go through the French. We'll also have to make sure that whatever and however we share doesn't reveal the source. That means we'll have to make it look like it's coming from multiple sources. Too many leads coming out of Paris might prompt the Russians to take a look at personnel who have served there in the past."

Protection of sources and methods. This is a phrase familiar even to the public, but they probably think it's just a cop-out or an evasion to conceal evil deeds. In reality it embodies a cardinal rule for the human intelligence operator – the life of the agent is sacred. Field officers have a very personal obligation to their agents. I was glad to see that Langley intended to protect Barsikov, even though we were not running him actively.

"That makes sense," I said.

"Good. One of your tasks now is to convince the French that it's a good idea. Do you think they'll agree?"

"We can count on their discretion. But they do have this axe to grind with the Brits."

Graham moved some lettuce around with his fork. "We can't ignore our obligations to our most important ally."

"I know. But we could cave to Picard on the *Al Sakir* thing; let him have his fun while we figure out how to handle all the rest. It would buy us time."

We paused while the waiter cleared the table and brought coffee and dessert, in this case bread pudding *à la mode.*

"It will be your job to convince the French that we're right."

"I'll do my best to make them think it was their idea to begin with."

Graham actually smiled.

"There is more," he said.

I was all ears.

"The White House isn't content with defensive measures only. The President is determined to see the Soviet Union on the ground with his foot on Gorbachev's neck. The Barsikov dossier may be the best weapon in our arsenal because it demonstrates the true weaknesses of the USSR. We have their shopping list, and that means we should be able to take advantage of it."

I was beginning to get the drift. "The active measures you mentioned before."

Graham nodded and shoved his dessert to the

side. The ice cream had melted while we talked. "We take advantage of the VPK's own program and toss some sand into their gears that will slow them down and cost them dearly."

I liked the sound of that.

"These operations, of course, will be tightly held. There will be only one field operative involved. Langley will prepare the material, and you'll be working with the liaison services and private companies selected for these operations."

Chapter 19

Geneva, Switzerland

James Abbot peered through the wooden double doors into the dining room that had been set up for the conference. He spotted the representatives from Vickers Shipbuilding Systems, GEC, and Westland, the company selling Blackhawk helicopters. Off in a corner stood Mohammed Attar, his elfin figure nearly concealed behind a potted plant, discrete as always, observing the crowd.

In fact, they were in the Prince's lavish Geneva villa on the shore of *Lac Genève*. There was no one in sight who was not an active participant in the bribes required to keep *Al Sakir* on track, over a dozen executives, in all. Most of them were quite enthusiastic about it all. They stood in small groups, shooting nervous glances over one another's shoulders. The absence of alcohol undoubtedly added to their unease.

To throw the press off the track the Prime Minister had decreed that no one of ministerial rank should attend, and the British side was led by Lord Crowley, head of the Defense Export Services Organization, the DESO, and his deputy. British Aerospace, of course was there in the person of the head of the Tornado Division. Well over a dozen people were in attendance at the conclave, the purpose of which was to conclude the *Al Sakir* negotiations and determine the form for all the related "side deals." Abbott was confident that the details of the negotiations would never see the light of day.

Everyone was waiting for the arrival of Prince

himself. The purpose of the meeting was to nail down the final details of exactly who would pay how much to whom and how they would conceal the transactions. Abbot's old friend, Mohammed Attar, was key to all this. He controlled the Swiss bank account into which the bribe money was to be deposited. The rate allegedly was to be three to ten percent of the value of the contracts. With Mohammed serving as Saudi bag man and Abbot working on the British side to ensure that the deal went through, they and the Prince stood to make a great deal of money.

Standing discretely in the corners of the room and in the hallway outside, were anonymous security men from MI-6. There were easily visible bulges under their coats.

A full hour after the Prince had promised to arrive, a procession of large, black automobiles pulled up to the entrance. There was a stretch limousine, with Mercedes sedans in front and behind. Large, dark men in business suits with snub barreled machine pistols suspended from straps over their shoulders poured out of the sedans and looked suspiciously in all directions before one of them opened the door of the limo for the Prince to step out.

The Prince was a confident man. He and Mohammed Attar alone would represent the Saudi side, that is, the main bribe recipients' side. Abbot was there in his capacity as the Prime Minister's personal representative. The whole scene reminded him of a feudal lord receiving tribute from his vassals. Abbot liked being on the side of the feudal lord, albeit secretly.

The Prince swept into the room in full Saudi regalia. His floor-length *thobe* was snow white, as was the *ghutra* affixed to his head by a black *iqal*. His beard was dyed jet black. He had a thick neck and double chin, and the flowing *thobe* could not conceal the corpulent figure of the dark complexioned Saudi prince. His girth was in the XXXL range.

The Prince's guards glared at the MI-6 security detail, and the MI-6 guys glared right back.

Abbot wondered what went through the minds of the security men as they observed negotiations that would enrich the men at the table beyond the wildest dreams of civil servants. Then again, it had been the Prime Minister herself who had insisted on their presence. They would be her eyes and ears. He must play his role well as HRH's representative.

James Abbott returned from Switzerland a jubilant man, fully confirmed in the expectation that he would soon come into a large fortune. That fortune would be in the form of illicit funds derived from so-called "commissions" on the biggest arms deal in history – *Al Sakir*. The deal was officially valued at over 20 billion pounds sterling. A large portion of that sum would be in the form of "prince's oil" that the British government would sell to pay the vendors. And much of the money that would be forthcoming from the Saudis to the British Defense industry would find its way right back into the pockets of the Prince and other influential royals who had involved themselves in the matter, as well as those lucky enough – like James Abbott – to belong to the exclusive "club" of *Al Sakir* insiders.

The extent of the corruption surprised even Abbott, permeating as it did every aspect of the deal, condoned by the Prime Minister herself, who would stop at nothing to secure the future health of the British arms industry. Abbott was unworried by the possibility that his own part in the scheme of kick-backs and outright bribes would be discovered. There were too many high ranking people involved, from the Prime Minister on down, for anyone in power to risk a hint of scandal.

Unbeknownst to him, however, events were conspiring on the other side of the world that would have a devastating impact on his sense of invulnerability.

Chapter 20

Moscow

Stepan Timofeyevich Barsikov parked his aging Lada in a space near his apartment building on *Ulitsa 1812*, named for the battle immortalized by Tchaikovsky. Only a few hundred meters away was the Battle of Borodino Museum with its circular panorama.

The apartment was on the fifth floor and was relatively upscale. The family had been rewarded with the apartment following Stepan's successful tour in Paris, when he was still on the way up the KGB ladder. It now served as a bitter reminder that his ascent had been stalled mid-way and would never resume.

Natasha was not at home when he arrived. It was late, after 7:00 PM, but his wife's absence did not surprise him. She had progressively spent less and less time at home over the past several months, and Barskikov was perfectly aware that she preferred the company of her current lover to his. Vodka and the occasional bottle of brandy now comforted his evenings.

They had enjoyed a close and loving relationship until the forced return from Canada and Barsikov's professional disgrace had transformed him from an outgoing, jovial man to the introverted and depressed person he had become. Natasha was an attractive blonde. She was a former Olympic gymnast and retained the looks and winsome body of her youth. She had always been attractive to men.

Stepan's own infatuation with Elena Trofimovna had coincided with the beginning of Natasha's infidelity, and he could not be certain which came first. It really made little difference to him. Fate had turned against him and fell upon him in waves of depression of ever increasing strength as he lost control of his life. Thank God, he thought, they had no children.

Stepan's life now centered on only one thing – his desire to do as much damage as possible to the organization that had betrayed him. Natasha's betrayal was dwarfed by the KGB'S perfidy. They had effectively stolen his future.

They had thrown him on the scrap heap with the other rejects of the service while the sons of the *Nomenklatura* who had no qualifications other than their names were given plum assignments abroad. The system was rotten to the core.

Ironically, his relegation to Department 'K's' analysis unit placed at his disposal its most important and closely held information.

He had been tossed aside by the KGB, his wife, and now Elena. Betrayal begets betrayal. By passing to the French every scrap of information to which he had access, he would have his revenge.

Chapter 21

Warsaw, 1974

As day two of their interrogation ground slowly to an end, the two young men once again faced Kowałczyk across the desk.

The Captain said, "I've had enough of your stalling and lies. Either sign your confessions immediately, or you will both be sent to prison to await trial. Your trial could well be delayed for many months. There is no hope for you."

He pointed to two typed documents that lay on the desk in front the prisoners. They were neatly typed in Polish, and neither Wafiq nor Mohammed had the slightest idea what they said.

Wafiq's once handsome face was covered with small cuts and crusted blood, there was blotchy bruising around both eyes, and his nose had swollen to twice its normal size. They both now wore loose fitting prison uniforms, beige with horizontal black stripes. Mohammed had not received as much physical punishment, but psychologically he was a wreck. He could not help thinking about how the trip to Warsaw had been his idea. Wafiq had come along only to please his friend and have a little innocent fun. Mohammed blamed himself for their predicament. He had never been particularly brave, but now he came to a decision.

Mohammed broke the silence, his voice barely a whisper, "Captain, sir, I will sign your confession, but my friend is completely innocent. He did nothing. He was nowhere near the girl when she went through the window. All of this is my fault. I will sign, but you must let my friend go."

Wafiq's head snapped around toward Mohammed. "My brother, you cannot do this. Someone must know where we are. They will not abandon us."

Mohammed shook his head sadly. "No one will ever find us in this hell hole," he said. "It's better that one of us gets out to carry the news to our families. It is only right that you go, Wafiq. This was my fault."

His powerful political and family connections would make it a problem for Kowałczyk to hold the Saudi much longer; the Lebanese was another matter. It already had been decided that the Saudi would be set free and deported, but Kowałczyk had skillfully used him as leverage against his companion. He wanted a signed confession, and now he would get one.

Pretending he was pondering a difficult decision, Kowałczyk instructed the guard to uncuff Mohammed's hands.

"If you sign the confession now, right at this moment," he said, "I give you my word that your friend will be expelled from Poland immediately."

He slid the single-spaced document, typewritten in Polish, towards the skinny Lebanese who was clearly frightened out of his mind.

Wafiq said quickly in Arabic, "Mohammed, it's a trick. Everything they say here is a lie. Don't sign it!"

But Mohammed had made up his mind, "You will go free now, my brother and friend. If I must die a martyr at the hands of these infidels, I would rather that you live to tell the story."

With that he grabbed the pen and slashed his signature across the bottom of the document. He slumped back into the chair and sobbed. His life, he knew, was over.

Chapter 22

Wafiq's clothing and other belongings were returned to him and he was allowed to wash and dress. Mohammed had been led immediately out of the interrogation room after signing the confession, and Wafiq had not seen him since. The young Saudi, his face now heavily bandaged, was hustled to Okęcia International Airport where his documents were returned and he was placed on an Air France non-stop flight to Paris.

Two days later, Poland's Deputy Minister of Internal Affairs, Władislav Pozoga, was surprised by the unexpected arrival at his office of the "senior partner" representative. The "senior partner" was the KGB, and its liaison mission in Poland was headed by grizzled veteran General Vitaliy Grigorievich Pavlov. He had been appointed to the post by Yuriy Andropov in 1973, and he had had his hands full ever since. Relations between the Polish SB and the KGB were not all sweetness and light.

Pavlov kept himself very well informed of Polish intrigues and political intentions, especially a burgeoning unofficial opposition movement. He had a network of reliable informants salted throughout the Polish Government, especially the intelligence services, that provided him information out of purely ideological motives, and he had the unconditional trust of his boss,

Andropov.

Pozoga supervised the activities of the Polish Intelligence Services, some of which were very gingerly directed against the Soviets. An unannounced visit from the old wolf Pavlov, therefore, did not please Pozoga. Conversations with the Russians were seldom cordial. And so it was with some trepidation that Pozoga stubbed out the odiferous cigarette he had been smoking and walked around his desk to greet the visitor. He noted with interest that the General was accompanied by his senior Aide, Lt. Colonel Yuriy Ivanovich Morozov, a hirsute bear of a man and another veteran of the KGB's Foreign Intelligence First Chief Directorate.

They formally shook hands all around, and Pozoga indicated they should take seats at the conference table along one side of his office. Thin morning light filtered through the milked window glass highlighting the blue wisps of tobacco smoke that hung layered in the air. Pozoga called his secretary and instructed her to bring them coffee.

"What can I do for you today, Comrade General?" asked Pozoga as the three took seats around the table. He spoke in Russian, a language he felt lacked sophistication and subtlety in comparison with his native Polish.

Pavlov came right to the point. "It's about the Saudis your people have in custody in connection with a death at the Forum Hotel," he said.

Pozoga was familiar with the matter. They had kept it out of the papers, but the rumor mill in Warsaw was full of lurid, mostly inaccurate accounts of what had happened. The most popular rumor was that a gang of drunken Arabs had purposely tossed a prostitute out of a fourteenth story window to her death. For this reason, the Deputy Minister had kept better track of progress than would normally be the case for common criminal activities.

"Only one of the men arrested was Saudi," he said carefully. "The other is Lebanese. This is a common criminal matter, Comrade. What is your interest?"

Pavlov regarded the Pole, a hint of distaste shading his face, pulling down the corners of his wide mouth. "Is it possible that you have failed to see the opportunity this situation offers?"

Pozoga had no idea what the Russian was talking about, but he was instantly on alert. "Opportunity? What are you talking about?"

Pavlov sighed heavily and turned to Morozov. "Yuriy Grigor'ich, will you please explain to the Deputy Minister?"

Morozov intoned, "Saudi Arabia is a very difficult target to penetrate, Comrade Deputy Minister. The fact that you hold these men in custody charged with a capital crime is a stroke of luck. With such leverage, we should be able to recruit them. We need assets inside 'The Kingdom,' and this is a unique opportunity."

Pozoga sat in silence for a few beats, considering how he would break the news to the Russians. *Damn them. This is none of their affair.* At the same time, he realized that this was an idea that his own intelligence people should already have been working on.

"This is a matter for our justice system, Comrades," he said carefully. "A young woman, a mere girl, was brutally murdered." Pozoga knew he was holding a weak hand, and this argument was as insubstantial as a tissue for the Russians.

Pavlov was not to be put off. "The security of the State must at times supersede 'justice,'" he said. "To put it bluntly, we want you to hand these two over to us."

"That is not possible, Comrade General" said Pozoga. *Jesus, I hate these arrogant bastards,* he thought. *How can I stave off the embarrassment?* He needed another cigarette badly.

Morozov leaned menacingly across the table, the Russian bear stretching his clawed paw across the Polish plain, "Come, come, *comrade*," he emphasized the word, "Surely we can work something out ... amicably."

Pozoga didn't like the implication. "There is something else, *comrade* General," he said, addressing his words to Pavlov. "Only one of the two arrestees remains in custody. The Saudi national was deported two days ago." He could not help adding, "Your sources are apparently not so well informed."

Pavlov's face infused with blood. "Comrade Deputy Minister," he said through his teeth, "if you still believe it is in your interest to maintain amicable relations with the KGB, I suggest you adopt a less nationalistic attitude." On more than one occasion Pavlov had expressed the view that Pozoga and many of his colleagues were more Polish than they were Communist.

Pozoga retorted with some asperity, "'Amicable relations,' as you term them, Comrade General, seem to consist of the SB providing the KGB with all the intelligence it collects, but receiving in return precious little of value."

Pavlov turned to Morozov. "Yuriy Grigor'ich, is it not true that we plan to share some valuable encryption technology with our SB brethren?"

"Yes, Comrade General. The equipment is scheduled to be turned over next week."

Pavlov turned back to Pozoga. "Do you think this brotherly exchange should take place?"

What Pozoga knew, but the KGB General hopefully did not, was that SB technicians were standing by to replace the encryption keys in the equipment the General had described. This would for the first time make it possible for Polish Intelligence to transmit encrypted messages that the Russians could not read. Pozoga knew that this would come as an unpleasant surprise for the KGB – something he would have to deal with at a later date. The Poles could not afford to lose the opportunity, and Pozoga had no choice but to cave to the Russian's demand.

"As I said, Comrade General," he said, adopting a more conciliatory if not quite groveling tone, "the Saudi national has been released and deported. Of what use could the Lebanese possibly be?"

"What do you think, Yuriy Grigor'ich?" Pavlov raised an eyebrow at Morozov.

"I think we have nothing to lose and possibly a great deal to gain. The Lebanese obviously is close to the Saudis. It was a grave error to release the Saudi," he said, with a stern glance in Pozoga's direction that made Pavlov smile. "But we should examine what we have left and see if there is any ore still to be mined here. If the Lebanese proves useless or refuses to cooperate, we can always hand him back to Polish 'justice.'"

Pavlov stood abruptly, and the others followed suit. Striding to the door, the General paused and said without looking back at Pozoga, "Have all the files on this case delivered to me personally not later than three o'clock this afternoon." He pushed his way through the door. "Good day -- Comrade."

When the Russians had gone, Pozoga immediately returned to his desk and rang his secretary. Lighting a much needed cigarette, he instructed her to have the officer in charge of the Forum Hotel case report to him immediately with all his files. *Whoever the idiot is,* he thought, *he'll soon find himself directing traffic in Poznan!*

Chapter 23

Paris

I was back at *No. 2, Place des Saussaies.* Picard sat at his desk beaming at me as though I had handed him the winning ticket to the national lottery. "My friend, Harry," he said, "Luck has smiled upon us. Our sources tell us that the Saudi Crown Prince plans a visit to Paris – one of his numerous 'shopping' trips to the City of Light. He's reserved rooms at the Ritz."

The Imperial Suite of the Ritz Hotel suited the Prince well. The richness of its 18th century décor and the vivid red and gold upholstered furniture appealed to his sense of propriety and self-importance. The $15,000 per day that the venerable establishment charged for the three bedroom suite was of little consequence to the Prince. So little, in fact, that his entourage was similarly housed in three other of the hotel's so-called "prestige suites."

Jacques Picard and I strode toward the hotel's main entrance across the cobblestoned expanse of the *Place Vendome*, its colonnaded buildings gilded sumptuously by the sunshine of the late summer afternoon. Atop the column in the center of the square, the statue of Napoleon Bonaparte as a Roman emperor cast its shadow over us. I loved the richness of this vibrant city, so imbued with history and culture. But now I was focused on the job at hand.

Entering the marbled foyer, we informed the concierge that we had an appointment with the Prince, and waited for one of the Saudi's factotums to escort us. When the man arrived, we both displayed credentials that identified us as officials of the *Dirección de la Surveillance du Territoire.*

It had not been difficult for me to convince Picard to agree to this plan. In turn, the Frenchman was able without too much resistance to persuade his superiors at the DST to provide the credentials for me. The French authorities were favorably inclined toward damaging British relations with the Saudis, and I had proposed a way to do so, but hopefully not mortally damaging British interests and American ones. That's why I wanted to tag along.

"The provenance of the information is the key," I had explained to Picard several days earlier. "Coming from other than an official source, I don't think it would be believed. And the Prince is not likely to agree to a meeting with some stranger off the street."

"Do you think this will stop the Saudis from buying from the Brits?"

"No. Things have progressed well beyond the point where it can be stopped altogether. Too much money already has changed hands both above and below the table. Promises have been made. Saudi flight crews are already being trained in England."

Picard shook his head, his mouth turned down in disgust and disappointment. "Then of what use would such an action be?"

I thought I knew the French heart well and was prepared with an answer.

"Scandal," I said, "a tremendous scandal. We know that there is a huge amount of corruption associated with *Al Sakir,* even within the British Government. At the very least, if we're successful, some of this will become public and there will be considerable fall-out. I'm certain you could convince the French press to cooperate, and there are elements of the British press that will jump all over it, *The Guardian* in particular. The British Government will be embarrassed. Politicians will lose their posts. Some might go to jail. The sale will proceed, but you can exact a measure of revenge."

"Revenge," The Frenchman repeated the word slowly, testing its taste and texture on his tongue. "It's a tempting idea."

I pressed the point. "There are no guarantees, but the Saudis would certainly be very grateful, maybe even grateful enough eventually to increase their arms purchases from France, perhaps even substitute some of the compromised *Al Sakir* acquisitions for purchases from you. After all, some of the British weapons systems they intend to acquire have been compromised."

"Now you're on the right track," said Picard, warming to the idea. "This is a convincing argument."

The Prince made us wait in the foyer of the plush Ritz suite for an "appropriately respectful" twenty minutes before we were ushered into the royal presence. For this meeting the Prince had chosen to wear the traditional Saudi *thawb*, a loosely fitting, black full length garment with a gold border, and a white *ghutra an iqal* on his head, secured by a black band. He was seated on an impressive brocaded sofa in the middle of the salon, his considerable bulk taking up most of the space, and did not rise when we entered. He gestured regally for us to be seated opposite him.

The Prince was Governor of Saudi Arabia's oil rich Eastern Province, a position that provided a lot of power.   It was well known that he subscribed to a principle shared by most of the large group of Saudi princes: *"Grab as much as you can as soon as you can."* There were a lot of Saudi princes; the Kingdom itself amounted to little more than a family business.

The Prince was greedy, but not especially stingy. In the course of his many trips to the West he was known to spend millions in a single day, and he was extremely generous to those who served him. He could not sustain such a lifestyle were it not for graft – his penchant for "commissions" from those who wished to do business in his country was well-known.

"I'm curious about the reason the DST asked for this meeting." The Prince spoke English, a language he had perfected during his college days at the University of Southern California. "I hope you don't mind speaking English."

"Not at all, your Royal Highness," began Picard. "I'm grateful for the opportunity to speak with you. But I'm afraid I bring information that may cause you some distress. It's precisely because this information directly concerns your Royal person and could cause you some personal discomfort that I am here."

Several thoughts crossed the Prince's agile mind. He could think of several hundred matters that could be embarrassing to one degree or another should they become public. He wondered which one the French had stumbled upon and waited for Picard to continue. The Prince's mustache twitched with mild curiosity. *How much will it cost to keep this quiet?*

Picard withdrew a sheaf of photocopies from the briefcase he carried and laid them on the coffee table.

"What's this?" asked the Prince, not deigning to

pick up the documents. He gestured for the assistant standing behind his chair to examine them.

Picard responded. "Your Highness. These documents provide details of certain weapons systems to be delivered to your country by the British - very sensitive information. Each document here has a cover sheet indicating that it was provided to you personally."

The Prince looked up at his assistant who was perusing the documents and who nodded in confirmation. Puzzled because he had never asked for nor received such documents from the Brits or anyone else, the Prince asked, "Are you telling me that you have stolen these documents from the British?"

"No, sir," said Picard. "We obtained these documents from a source in the Russian Intelligence Service, the KGB. The same source reported that the details of the weapons systems your country is buying from Great Britain are being given to the Iranian government by the Russians. We believe this threatens your country's national security."

The Iranian ploy was my idea. The Sunni Wahabis had no love for their belligerent Shiite neighbors.

The Prince was a not unintelligent man. He was quite aware of the threat posed to his country by the Iranian "apostates." He was also suspicious because he understood that the French would do anything they could to spoil the Saudi-British arms deal.

"Why don't you tell the British that they have a leak?"

"I'm afraid there's worse to come, sir. Given the fact that the documents in question are associated closely with you, indeed were apparently intended for you personally, there could be serious repercussions should it become public that they were given to the Russians. That's why we are here. We're certain the leak is from someone very close to you, a trusted person within your own entourage."

"Impossible!"

"I'm sorry to say that it's very possible, sir, in fact true," persisted Picard as he prepared to drive the nail in the coffin. "We believe that when you check the facts you will find that it could only someone in your entourage directly involved in the British deal."

An hour later, our business with the Prince concluded, we exited the hotel and crossed to the arcade on the other side of the *Place Vendome*. We decided to walk back to DST Headquarters and turned towards the Seine and then west on the *Rue de Rivoli* as we talked. Picard had left the sheaf of incriminating documents with a disturbed and angry Prince.

"I'd say that someone's goose is cooked," I said.

My French companion was not so sure. "He might be able to talk his way out of it."

"He won't last long under Saudi interrogation."

"It was your idea to suggest to the Prince that he should 'invite' the suspects to accompany him back to Riyadh to sort things out."

"And of you, Jacques, to assure him that the French authorities would not interfere, even if the suspects objected."

Mortal decisions are a part of intelligence work. We do all in our power to protect our own sources. When it comes to the sources of the enemy, however, there is no such obligation. There is no pity for enemy spies, unless, of course, we can double them back against their masters.

Nevertheless, I felt a twinge when I thought about what awaited these guys in Riyadh. I'm only human.

Chapter 24

Mohammed's Journey

When Mohammed Attar miraculously reappeared in Paris two weeks after Wafiq al Salah's expulsion from Poland, his Saudi friend had been overjoyed. Upon his own release, Wafiq had flown immediately to Riyadh to engage the aid of his cousin, Prince Saud, the Saudi Foreign Minister, to secure the release of his friend but had received no news whatsoever. When Mohammed called him from Paris, Wafiq boarded another flight to go and personally escort his friend back to Riyadh.

Mohammed professed ignorance of the reason for his unexpected release, and the two friends speculated that Saudi diplomatic pressure had been more effective than had been expected. In any event, Wafiq could never forget the debt he owed Mohammed for his selfless declaration of guilt in that Polish interrogation room. From that day forward Wafiq ensured that Mohammed Attar would never want for anything.

Out of both gratitude and guilt he secured a position for his friend as personal assistant to his cousin, the son of the Saudi King. In such a position his friend would never want for money. Over the years Attar had thrived and prospered, becoming the Prince's main "fixer," which meant that he travelled with the Prince, made living arrangements for him, and was responsible for handling the vast sums of money the Prince received as "commissions" or outright bribes.

Not to put too fine a line on it, he was the Prince's bag man.

Mohammed Attar did not regret the harm his spying for the Russians might do to the British or the Saudis. He especially despised the Royal family and all its hundreds of "princes," and most specifically his disgusting employer.

When he had first been inducted into the Prince's entourage thanks to the intercession of his friend he had been thrilled. Most of the friends of his youth had been Saudis, thanks to his mother's influence. He considered Wafiq Al-Salah as a brother, someone for whom he had been willing to sacrifice his life.

Any illusions Mohammed might have had that all Saudis were like Wafiq, however, had been quickly shattered by his association with the Prince.

The secret shame he carried over his agreement with the KGB led him to question many things. The carefree, fun-seeking young man he had been disappeared forever and the sycophancy of his former relationships with his Saudi friends was replaced by circumspection. Most important of all, Mohammed had turned to religion as a way to assuage his guilt. He had not done this in any spectacular fashion, but rather quietly, at first by studying the Qur'an on his own, and then regular attendance at one of Riyadh's many mosques.

His Saudi friends viewed this as a positive development and attributed it to Mohammed's gratitude to Allah for his delivery from the infidels.

Less than a month after the Polish nightmare, in December 1974, the Soviets invaded Afghanistan, an aggression against a Muslim nation that infuriated many Saudis, especially the young. Mohammed had become enamored of the works of Hassan al-Banna and even more so those of Sayyid Qutb of the Muslim Brotherhood. Qutb especially demanded the imposition of *Sharia* through *Jihad*. Of supreme importance in Mohammed's final epiphany had been his acquaintance with the son of a fabulously wealthy Saudi family, a true sheik, who also hated the Saudi royals.

As his religious devotion deepened, so did his detestation of the Prince and his sinful ways. The fat Prince travelled widely and frequently to the West where he controlled companies and owned many properties. He had his finger in every pie, collecting vast amounts of wealth through graft and corruption.

For some reason he trusted Mohammed Attar from the beginning, and the young man soon found himself enmeshed in the Prince's most secret and intimate interests. He was expected to arrange for the Prince's travel and handle all his personal contacts. He followed the Prince's orders to arrange for prostitutes whenever he travelled to the West and had personally witnessed the fat Saudi's depravities. His revulsion turned quickly into an abiding hatred for the entire Saudi royal family and all it represented.

He did not mind in the least passing Saudi secrets to the Russians. He rationalized that they would use the information to harm the sinful royal family in some way. But the Russian invasion of a Muslim land ended the accommodation he had made with his own conscience. He felt that he had betrayed not only the profligate Saudi royals, but also his deepest beliefs to infidels determined to destroy that which he held dear.

Mohammed arrived at a fateful decision. He would confess his crimes and offer his neck to the executioner's blade, perhaps thus atoning for his sins. If permitted by some miracle to live, he would leave Saudi Arabia to join with the mujahedeen fighting the Russians in Afghanistan. His new mentor, the Sheik, was deeply involved in financing and sending fighters to face the Russians.

And so it was that Mohammed tearfully confessed the perfidy of his KGB affiliation to the Sheik, prostrating himself before the tall, dark-skinned firebrand, and placing himself at his mercy. He divulged everything, from the sinful events of the evening leading to his and Wafiq's arrest in Warsaw, to the stark choice presented to him by the KGB.

The Sheik had said nothing for several minutes, his long, ascetic face a placid mask, his eyes closed in contemplation. Finally he spoke, and Mohammed would never forget that mellifluous, kind voice as the Sheik forgave him, even praised him for having the courage to confess. His mentor told him to rise and sit beside him. Tears coursed down Mohammed's face as he grasped the Saudi's hand and kissed it repeatedly.

The Sheik did not accept Mohammed's request to be sent to Afghanistan. No, there was a more important mission, and Allah, Blessed be His name, had sent Mohammed Attar to carry it out. The Sheik's most fervent desire was to overthrow the corrupt House of Saud and the entire extended family that brought nothing but shame to the Land of the Prophet, and Attar was perfectly positioned to assist. Rather than become a rifle-carrying mujahedeen, Mohammed was to become a fighter of a different sort, preserving his association with the Russians and deepening his relationship with the Prince. He could thus be of greatest service as a source of information and influence that the Sheik would put to use when the time was ripe.

It was with a clear conscience and a well-defined sense of purpose that Mohammed Attar left his apartment on his way to a meeting with James Abbot. Afterwards, he would head to Heathrow to catch a flight to Paris. Unaware of the events that had placed him at the intersection of KGB and CIA interests, he had been summoned there unexpectedly by a call from the Prince's secretary that very morning.

He stepped out of a taxi and hurried up the steep steps to the Italianate entrance of the Reform Club in Pall Mall. He was late for the meeting with James Abbott.

He announced himself to the porter, who pointed to Abbot who was chatting with another member in the club's spectacular multi-storied atrium. Attar waited at a respectful distance until Abbott spotted him and broke off his conversation to greet the diminutive Lebanese gentleman.

"You're just in time for lunch, old man," he said. "Shall we move into the Coffee Room?" This room, located on the club's ground floor, served as a members' restaurant and a place where guests were permitted.

"Certainly," replied Attar, "With pleasure."

As they crossed the marbled expanse of the atrium, the Lebanese reflected wryly on the irony of Abbott's belonging to a club that touted its criteria for membership as "character, talent, and achievement."

He did not look forward to the meal, not because of Abbott's smarmy company, but because he found the Club's food abominable.

Once seated at the otherwise unoccupied end of one of the long common tables, a predictably unappetizing salad consisting of wilted lettuce, a few slices of cucumber and a wedge of rock-hard tomato in front of him, Attar announced that he would be absent from London for a short time. "The Prince has invited me to visit him in Paris. He's there for a short stay."

The use of the word "invited" was a euphemism. When the Prince "invited" Attar into his presence, it was a command. The two had developed an easy relationship over the years, but when the Prince asked Attar to do something, the Lebanese had learned that alternative courses of action were unacceptable.

Abbott was unconcerned. "Ah, gay Paree. You're a lucky man, Mohammed. I hope you'll remember me to the Prince."

"I suspect you'll be seeing him again soon yourself," said Attar.

"What's the reason for your trip?"

Attar surveyed the space around them and lowered his voice. "*Al Sakir*, I should think. He probably wants my reading of the Geneva meeting. I am informed that the Prime Minister has arranged for the credits required for the purchase to go forward." He referred to Wafiq al Salah's recent conversation with the Prime Minister.

Abbott was ecstatic at this news. "So, the money will start to flow at last!"

The Minister of State for Defense Procurement

was not referring strictly to an exchange of funds between the British and Saudi governments, Attar knew.

"Yes," he replied drily, "I am certain of that."

"Excellent!"

"When do you leave for Paris?"

"This afternoon."

Abbott finished his bangers and mash with exultant gusto, completely oblivious to the disgust the dish aroused in his companion. Attar shoved the less than presentable lettuce around his plate, anxious to be on his way.

He hoped the Russians would soon recruit Abbott so that he would no longer have to deal with the avaricious Brit.

At Heathrow, Attar was surprised to find Wafiq al Salah waiting in the First Class lounge to board the same flight to Paris.

"Wafiq, what are you doing here?"

"The Prince called and asked me to come see him." Al Salah smiled broadly at the sight of his old friend. "You too, I see."

Attar sighed theatrically, "Oh, yes. Summoned once again into his radiant presence. I wonder if he has developed a sudden requirement for French girls."

Wafiq's smile cooled a degree. "I don't think so, Mohammed. I think it's business."

"I don't know. The call just said to be there this evening."

"Well, we'll find out soon enough," said Wafiq as

they settled into their seats.

Three hours later a cab deposited them at the hotel entrance on the Place Vendome.

Chapter 25

The Prince received Wafiq and Mohammed warmly, inquired solicitously about Wafiq's family, and chatted with them for several minutes. He then unexpectedly announced that he wished the two to fly back to Riyadh with him that same day. Both Wafiq and Mohammed were taken aback by the unexpected request. Wafiq, with more independence than Mohammed, had protested that he had pressing matters awaiting him in London, but the Prince had dismissed his concern with a careless wave of his hand.

"You both will be in Riyadh tomorrow," he stated flatly, the warmth now absent from his voice. The presence of the Prince's bodyguards made it clear that this was an invitation not to be refused.

The flight was long and, at least psychologically uncomfortable for the two old comrades. The time was passed mostly in silence, given the all too obvious presence of guards on either side of them. The experience reminded them both too much of their Warsaw adventure fifteen years earlier, but still, Wafiq could conjure up no idea of what infraction they might have committed.

Mohammed appeared similarly nonplussed. There was big money at stake, and the Prince was notoriously greedy. Could this be about just money? That would not explain the presence of Wafiq al Salah, who didn't need the Prince's money. But the arms deal was the only commonality between them that involved the Prince.

They did not see the Prince again after Paris. When the plane landed, they were bundled down the rear boarding stairs straight into a waiting closed van. Emblazoned on its side was the symbol of the Saudi Ministry of the Interior.

They had been handed over to the notorious *mabahith*, the Saudi Secret Police.

The van ride did not last long, although neither had any idea of where they might be in the city. When the rear doors opened they saw that they were in a large courtyard, encircled by a high brick wall topped with razor wire. Despite their muddled protestations, they were shoved roughly across the courtyard and into a low building that stood opposite the electric gates through which the van had entered. They were issued prison garb and placed together in a locked room that was at least air conditioned, and both, now accustomed to the cooler clime of the United Kingdom, felt some relief from the stifling heat outside.

"What's going on, Wafiq?" Mohammed was the first to speak.

"I have no idea. I've done nothing to merit such treatment. If this has something to do with *Al Sakir*, they should know that had it not been for me, they would have no deal at all."

"Maybe he's after more money."

"Money!!!" Wafiq was suddenly indignant. "What can this have to do with money? Anything I am due to receive in connection with this is purely symbolic, and it's certainly not enough to provoke the Prince to such an extent. I've known him since I was a boy. This is unlike him."

"You've known him since you were a boy," repeated Mohammed, "but I've known him as a man. You know how he is these days – no amount of money is too small to escape his greed."

"I don't believe it," said Wafiq.

The interrogations began the following morning when four large men burst into the cell and without a word proceeded to punch and kick the two prisoners, pick them up and bounce them off the walls. This went on for about fifteen minutes, and then they were left alone, bleeding on the floor, gasping for breath.

Long hours passed, and then another day, before the four thugs paid a return visit, and the interrogations became serious. This time they carried canes, slender lengths of bamboo used in traditional punishments in The Kingdom. The two were taken to separate but adjoining cells where they were bound to tables flat on their stomachs and their feet secured in stocks. The canes came quickly into play. Wafiq had never felt such pain as when they began to beat the soles of his feet with the slender rods.

The baring of the soles of one's feet is particularly humiliating in Arab culture, and this added to the overall effectiveness of the punishment. Had sturdier implements been used, the two men could have been crippled for some time, if not for life. But as it was, their interrogators were following the orders of the Prince only to inflict enough pain to elicit confessions. In the absence of confessions, the punishment would increase in vigor. And it did.

The *mabahith* interrogators were well practiced in extracting information. They adopted the practice of torturing the two in turns, so that one could hear the cries of the other from the adjoining cell.

The bizarre questions put to him confounded Wafiq. Why did they keep asking about spying for the Russians? This was a ridiculous accusation.

Mohammed, of course, now understood why they had been taken. The Prince had somehow discovered his secret! From the next cell, he could hear the interrogators questioning Wafiq al Salah.

Mohammed experienced a dizzying sense of déjà vu. All those years ago when he had made a false confession to save his friend, his motive had been pure. Through his pain, or perhaps because of it, he now achieved clarity of thought, a sense of purpose that brought upon him a calmness that would have amazed his tormentors. He knew that the key was *purity*. He, the triple agent, was nevertheless *pure*. His motives were borne of devotion to Allah and a cause greater than himself. He knew what he had to do.

Over the cacophony of his own screams as the *mabahith* interrogator ripped out a second fingernail, Wafiq heard his friend's shout. "Wafiq is innocent! I'm the one you want."

What is he saying? Wafiq slipped into unconsciousness in the adjoining cell.

Chapter 26

When he awoke in darkness, chained again to the wall, Wafiq thought he was alone, but then he heard a soft, disembodied moan from somewhere across the room. "Mohammed?"

It was several moments before the answer came, floating like a fragile bubble in the darkness.

"Wafiq."

"What's going on? I thought I heard you say something before I passed out."

A deep sigh, then, "I did. I'm guilty of what they say."

"My brother, not again. You cannot sacrifice yourself again for me. We are both innocent of what they say. Try to be strong and resist the temptation to confess. It will not end the pain."

From out of the gloom emerged a gurgle that might have been a laugh, rising from deep within Mohammed's chest. "The pain is good. It clears the mind and prepares the way to Heaven. I will be a *shahid*, you know."

Mohammed's senseless babbling alarmed Wafiq. "Don't do this. It won't do any good. This is not Warsaw."

Again the soft, gurgling laugh.

"No, it is not Warsaw, my brother. It is Riyadh, the world's capital of corruption and vice. The Land of the Prophet ruled by apostates!"

"Mohammed, what are you saying?"

As much as he loved Wafiq al Salah, Mohammed had long ago despaired of his friend ever finding the True Path. Wafiq had been beguiled by the easy life his riches provided, had married an infidel and adapted to their ways. How could he ever understand? But he was still Mohammed's friend.

"I am saying that, yes, I have been an agent of the infidel Russians. It was the price to escape from Warsaw. But since then I have pursued a hidden course, the course of righteousness, the way of Allah, blessed be His name, which was opened for me. I shall die a martyr for Islam, my brother, not for the Russians, and my sins will be forgiven."

"The Russians? I don't understand."

Mohammed's words were contradictory – *had the torture driven his friend mad?*

"They made a proposition I could not refuse all those long years ago in Warsaw. It was my only escape from rotting in a Polish prison. I was young. I grasped the nettle, and they set me free."

Wafiq's mind was in turmoil. "I ... don't understand," was all he finally managed to say.

Out of the darkness: "My life is unimportant, my brother. I give it up gladly. You are guilty of many sins, but you are not guilty of the actions that brought us to this place, and you are still my brother."

The following day the guards removed Wafiq from the cell, leaving Mohammed behind.

"Farewell, my brother," the voice wafted out of the darkness behind him.

Wafiq was too overcome by emotion to reply.

They took him to an infirmary somewhere in the bowels of the *mabahith* prison where he was allowed to take a shower, and then they dressed his wounds. The clothes he had worn when he travelled from London to Paris were returned, cleaned and freshly pressed.

Barely able to walk on his bruised feet, he was helped out into the sunlight where a stretch Mercedes limousine was waiting in the courtyard, accompanied by two SUV chase cars filled with armed men. He found the Prince waiting inside the limousine.

"Wafiq, my dear cousin, you cannot know how much it disturbs me that you have been subjected to such treatment."

The Prince's voice betrayed no concern or repentance.

Wafiq said nothing, fearing what might come out of his mouth if he opened it. He was angry, deeply angry, and the object of his ire was sitting right there beside him, close enough to dig his fingers into the fat neck and strangle.

During the long final night in their shared cell, Mohammed Attar had bared his soul to his friend. From his unexpected encounter with KGB Colonel Morozov in Warsaw to the inspiration and forgiveness he had experienced from the Sheik and his discovery of true Islam. Securing his position with the Prince, something Wafiq had intended as a boon to his dearest friend, had soured Mohammed's soul. The Prince's greed, his debaucheries, everything about him had served only to shrivel Mohammed's spirit and drive him into the arms of dangerous fanatics. Wafiq respected his friend's deepening spirituality, which had been clear enough to see, but he had never suspected the extremes to which it had led him.

"I understand your silence," the Prince continued when he decided that no reply would be forthcoming from Wafiq. "But you must understand that everything you experienced at the hands of the *mabahith* was, unfortunately, necessary. The crimes committed by that Lebanese dog are detestable. They are transgressions against the very fabric that holds The Kingdom together and protects the Holy Cities. It was, after all, you who vouched for him and suggested him for my service. What was I to think? I had to be sure."

The Prince paused to light a cigarette. "The dog's own words have convicted him. Your cell was equipped with microphones, of course. We heard everything he said, and I ordered your immediate release. You'll be on a plane to London today -- one of my own planes. You are due every courtesy and the thanks of The Kingdom."

Wafiq nodded. There was nothing he could do. Right now, his overriding concern was to get out of The Kingdom. He hoped never to see it again.

Chapter 27

"Mohammed Attar has disappeared."

Picard and I sat at a small sidewalk table at a café on Boulevard St. Germain. Half-finished glasses of beer and the remains of sandwiches littered the table top. A week had passed since the meeting with the Prince.

"Well," I said, "I think we know where he is. According to your surveillance, he was picked up at Charles de Gaulle in a car owned by the Prince and driven straight to the Ritz. There was another man with him identified him as Wafiq al Salah, a high roller from London."

The DST had placed Attar and his companion under surveillance at Charles DeGaulle. When they arrived at the *Place Vendome* we observed Attar and Al Salah enter the hotel. Not long after, they were escorted out to a waiting limousine. The car took them to Orly Airport, south of the city, where a private jet was waiting. The plane's crew had filed a flight plan to Riyadh.

"That's the last time anyone has seen either man, as far as we know," said Picard. "Al Salah hasn't returned to London.

"I don't think we'll be seeing them again if I know the Saudis," I replied.

We clinked our glasses and drained the last of the beer. Then we ordered more beer, and I lit a cigar. I know that cigars are best not smoked in the open air, but it was a good day, and we were at *Les Deux Magots*.

I was certain recent days had not been so kind to

Attar and Al Salah.

But a week later, one of the two re-appeared, and we waited to see what would happen next.

Chapter 28

London

Becky Haversham al Salah was distinctly unhappy. Her husband had left for what he had assured her would be a short business trip to Paris two weeks ago, and she had heard not a word from him since. This was unlike Wafiq al Salah, and Becky was desperately concerned.

She had called the Ritz Hotel in Paris to inquire whether her husband was still there with the Prince but the hotel informed her that the royal party had departed unexpectedly to return to Saudi Arabia. Becky tried to convince herself that her husband had simply been unable to let her know of his plans and would be contacting her soon. But the phone refused to ring.

In her growing desperation, she had even placed a call to the odious Mohammed Attar's flat, but there was no answer.

Finally, Wafiq returned. Becky heard the crunch of wheels in the drive and ran to open the door in time to see him descend from an airport cab.

Despite the relief that fluttered her heart, her initial reaction was anger over his long, mysterious and frighteningly uncommunicative absence, but the words of reproach died on her lips as soon as she beheld her husband as he made his way painfully up the steps.

"Wafiq, what in the world?"

She ran to his side to support him when he staggered slightly. He put his arms around her and clung tightly, his body wracked by suddenly heaving sobs.

"My darling, I thought I'd never see you again." His words were liquid with tears. She had never seen him so emotionally distraught.

Barely able to stand, he leaned heavily upon her as they ascended the steps and entered the house as though his feet were unable to bear his own weight. She could not imagine what calamity had overtaken her handsome, urbane husband, but he looked like he had been through a war. His skin was sallow, and he had definitely lost weight. He seemed barely able to put one foot in front of the other, and his right hand was swathed in bandages.

Guiding him to a sofa she repeated, "Wafiq, what happened? Have you been in an accident? I've been so worried."

With a visible effort, her husband brought himself under control.

"I think I could use a whiskey." His voice was so low that Becky had to lean over him to understand what he was saying.

"Of course." She hurried to the drinks cabinet and poured a generous glass of scotch which Wafiq downed in a single swallow that brought on a fit of coughing.

"It was Mohammed," Wafiq's voice was still low, his eyes haunted. "I still can't believe it."

The despicable Mohammed Attar, of course.

"What, darling? What is it you can't believe?"

"Mohammed ...," his voice faltered. "He is a Russian spy. All these years ... ever since Warsaw. They thought I was involved, too."

None of this made sense to Becky. "Involved ...?

What are you talking about, Wafiq? Where have you been?"

Again, he shuddered. "The *mabahith*," he whispered, "the Saudi secret police."

He held out the empty glass, and Becky rushed to recharge it.

It took hours for her to pull the story out of him, painful bit by painful bit, and there were parts she was certain he still was not telling.

Chapter 29

There were very few people whose request for an unscheduled meeting would be accepted by the British Prime Minister, and Wafiq al Salah was one of them. He was a personal friend, a generous campaign contributor, and a key link in the biggest arms sale in history. Curious about the reason for the Saudi's unusual request, she swept into the reception room at No. 10 Downing St. to greet him. The handsome Arab stood as she entered, somewhat slowly and painfully, it seemed to her.

"I apologize," he said, displaying a bandaged hand, but I am unable to take your hand this morning."

She took in his appearance more carefully. He did not appear to be well.

"Wafiq, whatever has happened to you. Please sit down."

The man had been teetering slightly on his feet, and she was suddenly fearful that he might collapse.

"It's not as bad as it looks, Prime Minister – a slight accident is all."

She quickly took a seat herself so the obstinately courteous man would finally sit in her presence.

"Now sit here with me on the sofa, and tell me what brings you here – out of a sick-bed it would appear."

Wafiq essayed a smile, but she thought she detected sadness behind it. The man's eyes were full of pain.

He said, "My injuries are merely physical, Prime Minister, and they will heal quickly enough. But I have suffered a spiritual blow that I fear will not so easily be cured, and it is this that brings me to see you."

The Prime Minister knew this man well enough to realize instantly that whatever had brought him to Downing Street this morning must be of some direct concern to her. The reference to a "spiritual blow," however, mystified her. She was unused to being involved in the emotional problems of others.

"Why don't you start at the beginning," she said. "I'll have some tea brought in."

After the servant had deposited a silver tea service on the occasional table and retreated from the room, Wafiq began. "You will recall the story I told you a long time ago about my unfortunate encounter with the Polish authorities when I was a young man."

Al Salah's tale of brutality at the hands of communist thugs had been one of the things that had led her to trust the man. There was nothing, she believed, like being mugged to turn a liberal into a conservative. "Of course, Wafiq, but I don't see ..."

"I'll explain," uncharacteristically, Wafiq interrupted her.

The Prime Minister blinked and sat back, waiting. This was a man with a story to tell, and she received the impression that it was not inconsequential.

Before coming to Downing Street, Wafiq had tried to analyze his own motivations. What he would tell the Prime Minister could endanger the still fragile *Al Sakir* deal, but he calculated that things had progressed too far for the entire matter to collapse. The revelation of a Russian penetration at the heart of the negotiations, should it become public, would cause a public outcry, and could lead to further revelations of the corruption that greased the gears. The Saudis stood to lose, but

Wafiq no longer cared about his homeland and the tribe that controlled it, the same people who controlled the brutal *mabahith*. They represented a regime and a belief system that still moldered in the Middle Ages. Sadly, his lifelong friend, Mohammed, had become entangled not only with the Russians, but also with a group of equally unappetizing fanatics that, although opposed to the Saudi ruling family, were even more retrograde than they. The anger Wafiq had felt upon his release had continued to wax towards incandescence.

Wafiq had done nothing wrong. He knew this, but his anger was accompanied and fueled by borrowed guilt. Mohammed Attar was a traitor, yes; but his jailhouse confession had in some mysterious fashion shifted his traitor's burden to Wafiq, a burden that could be lifted only by confession, a peculiarly western concept. Perhaps revealing what his friend had told him would in some way absolve Mohammed of his sins. Knowledge was, indeed, a dangerous commodity, and he wanted to be rid of it. He would transfer the weight to the shoulders of someone better equipped to deal with it.

"That's where it all started – in Warsaw. We were just two boys out to have some fun, but it didn't turn out that way ..."

He told the story as Mohammed had told it to him in Riyadh: the recruitment by the KGB, the position with the Prince, the Sheik, and the tangled web that *Al Sakir* had become.

And Mohammed had told him about James Abbott – not only that worthy's pecuniary interest in the arms deal, but also the Russian interest in recruiting him.

When he had finished, Wafiq sat back, exhausted not so much by the telling as by the fact that the inexplicable guilt was still with him. Sharing deadly knowledge did not decrease its weight, he decided, but rather only compounded it as it passed from one person to another, leaving each with an equal load to bear.

The Prime Minister sat very still, her eyes never leaving her interlocutor as she considered what she had just heard. Finally, she asked, "Do you plan to share this information with anyone else, Wafiq?"

He looked up at her then, with evident surprise. "The Saudis, at least the Prince, already have this information, Prime Minister. I don't know what they intend to do about it, if anything. I believe his primary interest at this point is to keep *Al Sakir* on track. He will not want to lose his 'commissions,' of course. I don't think he's likely to do anything rash."

"Of course not." The Prime Minister knitted her brow as she turned over the various implications of what she had just learned.

Wafiq continued, "I just thought I should even the playing field by making sure you were aware of all the facts. I will certainly not tell anyone else. It is too shameful."

"Thank you, my dear friend," she said. "Your loyalty will not be forgotten. Are you still in any danger from the Prince or the Saudi government?"

She was genuinely concerned. Behind her calm façade she was horrified by the brutality to which Wafiq had been subjected in Riyadh and not for the first time was reminded of the medieval mindset of the Saudis.

Too bad they had all the money.

"I'll see to it that you and your family are protected until this has blown over."

"I don't think that's necessary, Prime Minister."

"Nonsense, we'll set some very capable guard dogs around you."

"Thank you," was all he could say.

She walked him to the street door of No. 10, an unusual courtesy for anyone who was not a head of state, and then returned to her office where she sat for several minutes, thinking. At last, she asked her secretary to summon the Head of MI-5 to Downing Street.

Wafiq al Salah pulled off his shoes and put his aching feet up on the leather ottoman. The bruises and scrapes received in Riyadh had healed, but he still suffered from the punishment the caning had inflicted on the soles of his feet. This was his quiet hour in his study when he read the papers and enjoyed the pre-dinner cocktail that Becky always prepared for him.

He was on page two of the *Times* when his attention was arrested by a short article below the fold, edged in black. His pulse quickened as he read it: "Government Minister Dies in Crash." The thought occurred to him that it was strange that such news should not be on page one.

The short article detailed the tragic accident that had taken the life of Minister of State for Defense Procurement James Abbott whose automobile had been broadsided by a train after it inexplicably stalled on a country rail crossing. The Prime Minister had issued a statement of condolence to the family.

Wafiq carefully laid the paper aside and leaned his head back to close his eyes. He had told the Prime Minister about Abbott's relationship with Mohammed Attar as well as the interest Russian Intelligence had in him.

Wafiq had divorced himself from further involvement in the corruption-filled deal that he himself had made possible, but he did not doubt that it would gain momentum and make fortunes. It had cost Mohammed Attar his life and robbed Wafiq of his equanimity. The underbelly of the Saudi regime was sordid and repugnant, and he was ashamed of the "royal" blood that flowed in his own veins.

As for James Abbott, he would never know what really happened, and he didn't want to.

We watched it unfold from our perch in Paris. There were numerous articles in the British press about the unexplained disappearance of Mohammed Attar. It was rumored that he had been seen on several occasions in the company of deceased Minister of State for Defence Procurement James Abbot. The more conspiracy minded of British scribblers tried to link the two events, and this led to increased scrutiny of the *Al Sakir* deal.

Picard and his colleagues followed all of this with undisguised glee, and I had no doubt that they were feeding tidbits of damning information to their contacts in the press. *Le Figaro* took the line that the entire arms deal was corrupt from top to bottom.

The hostile press led London opposition

politicians to open several inquiries that led eventually to serious discomfort in places like BAE and No. 10 Downing Street.

Despite French satisfaction, we still had the problem of how to disseminate Barsikov's information to affected allies without compromising the source. We made a good start on this with the French, but unforeseen events soon relieved us of that particular concern.

Chapter 30

Headquarters of the KGB First Chief Directorate - Yasenevo

The French refer to dusk, when it is impossible to discern shapes in the gathering gloom, as *entre loup et chien* 'between wolf and dog.'

Stepan Barsikov normally waited for the evening exodus of workers from Yasenevo to thin out before leaving the office. Thousands of people toiled in the modern, multi-story complex to keep the mechanism of the First Chief Directorate in motion. Most of them did not own an automobile, and special buses waited at the exit to carry them to the city center.

The sodium lights that illuminated the parking area were just coming on as Stepan exited the building. The compound, consisted of a central group of tall buildings, ancillary buildings, and a large section of special housing reserved for high-ranking officers. The heavily wooded surroundings had earned the compound the sobriquet "The Forest."

His meeting with the man at the monastery had been simultaneously frightening and exhilarating. Now he waited patiently, smug in his certainty that Lebedev's prize operation in London would soon unravel and with it the office chief's career. Stepan's world was all anticipation now as he waited for the axe to fall. Perhaps, he thought, Elena might even come back to him. Yes, she was sure to do so when the entire world beheld Lebedev's feet of clay.

He walked out of the north exit and turned right toward the metal gates of the vehicular entrance. The employees' parking lot was located just a few dozen meters north of the gates. Still, it was a bitch to walk even that short distance during the harsh Moscow winters. Summer was now well-established, however, and the air was redolent with the smell of pine from the surrounding woods. He was in a good mood.

The parking lot was rapidly emptying, and he had just unlocked his car when something, a distant sound that was somehow familiar, caught his attention. He looked around, uncertain what it had been. Then, there it was again – voices, the high-pitched tinkle of a woman's laughter. He scanned the lot and spotted Lebedev's car, a late model Volga, parked at the edge nearest the trees in a spot where the yellow glare from the overhead lights did not quite penetrate.

As he crept closer, circling around like a hunter so as to approach from the rear, the voices became more distinct as they escaped through a half open window. With a start, he recognized Elena's giggle. They didn't notice as he crept up behind them, and for good reason. Through the window Stepan could see that the girl's blouse was off, and Lebedev had his face buried in her breasts. He was making little doggie sounds, "Woof, woof," and Elena giggled more loudly with each woof.

Noiselessly, Stepan retreated to his battered Lada. He sat behind the wheel breathing heavily, trying to regain some sort of control, but he failed. His entire body trembled. A blind rage was building inside him, a rage that demanded release. All the weeks and months of his suffering, the ridicule of his fellow analysts, the way the KGB had betrayed him, the helplessness he had felt – all of this coalesced at this moment of crisis into white hot conviction. He was a pressure cooker that had reached its maximum limit. With mesmerizing clarity, he suddenly *knew* what he had to do. He wouldn't wait for the damned French to destroy his rival.

Stepan opened the glove compartment and removed the large hunting knife he always kept there. He again stealthily approached the rear of Lebedev's car, his face frozen now in a rictus of rage. Crouching below window level, he duck-walked to the passenger side door, his heart pounding. Elena's giggles increased, becoming interspersed with little moans of pleasure, enraging him still further.

Gripping the knife tightly he wrenched the door open. Elena yelped in surprise and Lebedev jerked up from between her legs, his head cracking painfully against the roof of the car.

Later, Stepan could remember only that there had been a lot of blood.

He lunged over the top of the girl and slashed savagely upward, catching the awkwardly positioned Lebedev in the neck with the sharp edge of the blade and then slashed again cutting into his arm. Lebedev instinctively recoiled from the knife.

Completely out of control now, Stepan turned his attention to Elena and plunged the eight inch blade deep into the girl's bare chest with such force that he buried it to the hilt. She stared at him with wild, surprised eyes and then her mouth gaped open with a soundless scream that forced the blood already gurgling in her throat out onto Barsikov. He continued stabbing frenziedly, repeatedly.

Lebedev had somehow managed to open the driver's side door and was on his hands and knees on the parking lot's macadam surface. Blood coursed from his sliced neck and through his fingers as he tried to staunch the flow.

Stepan was screaming now, an incoherent stream of epithets and gibberish as he continued to sink the blade into an already dead Elena. Lebedev somehow managed to get to his feet and half-ran, half-staggered towards the main gates. He was halfway there when Stepan finally looked up at spotted him.

With a feral growl he bolted after his prey. Stepan's hand and arm, indeed one whole side of his upper body was wet and dripping with gore. His face and hair were likewise soaked. His bulging eyes reflected madness in the yellow glare of the parking lot lights.

Lebedev heard him coming and found adrenalin-inspired strength to increase his speed. He began screaming now, a high-pitched, keening sound torn from his lacerated throat.

The gate guards looked up and were frozen for an instant by the macabre scene unfolding before them. Two men were rushing in their direction. Both covered in blood, one pursued by the other. The two guards, camouflage uniformed special troops, looked at one another in amazement and then reacted. The one nearest the guard shack pressed the alarm button and a klaxon sounded. This would put the security garrison on alert and bring reinforcements to the gate.

Until reinforcements arrived one of them had to remain on post while the other rushed forward, machine pistol at the ready. It was clear that the first man was being pursued by the other, and the pursuer was waving a large, bloody knife. The guard allowed the first man to pass him and then took up position to intercept the pursuer.

"*Stoi*," he shouted, "Halt! Halt or I'll fire!"

The man with the knife did not stop.

The guard released the safety on his weapon and fired a short burst, catching the Stepan in the legs.

He stumbled as his momentum carried him forward and down to the tarmac on his face. Gibberish continued to spew from his mouth as he tried to propel himself forward on his elbows, still clutching the knife, his shattered legs dragging behind. The guard assessed the danger as minimal and cautiously approached the fallen man, quickly kicking the knife from his bloody hand.

Stepan continued screaming as other guards arrived to surround him. He didn't stop screaming for a long time.

Chapter 31

Conference Room - Yasenevo

"Do you think he's telling the truth?" General Yuriy Ivanovich Morozov headed Directorate "S," responsible for KGB Illegals operations of the First Chief Directorate.

The General presided over a grim meeting on the third floor of the First Chief Directorate's headquarters. Across the expanse of a conference table he now faced a dozen KGB officials, but the person to whom he directed his question was a Colonel from Directorate "T," responsible for the clandestine acquisition of foreign technology.

"We have no way of knowing for certain," replied the Colonel. He had been asked this question many times and was very uncomfortable under the stormy eyes of General Morozov. "He appears to be completely insane. Imagine, such a thing happening right there on the grounds! One person dead and the other in the hospital."

The Colonel knew before he finished that his feeble attempt to divert attention from the main point was doomed and mentally kicked himself for the vacuity of the comment.

"'He appears to be completely insane,'" mimicked Morozov, "And no one noticed his condition until he made a shish kabob out of this woman and cut the throat of his section chief?"

Morozov was exasperated.

The Colonel sadly shook his head. "All members

of his analytical section are being questioned."

Morozov continued, "But this analyst, Barsikov, had complete access to Directorate 'T' and Line 'X' operations, even the identities of agents? How is this possible? You've confirmed it?"

Agent identities were supposed to be strictly compartmentalized from analysts, but the people of Directorate 'T' were for the most part former operations officers with appropriate clearances.

The Colonel squirmed in his chair. Without raising his eyes he replied, "Yes sir"

"What did Barsikov say, exactly?"

The General turned to the counter intelligence officer who had been in charge of Barsikov's interrogation.

"We didn't even have to persuade him to talk," he said. "As soon as we got him into a cell and shot him full of tranquilizers, he spilled everything – how he contacted the French, where and when he met with them at Kolomenskiy Park, and what he gave them. He certainly knew agent identities and even bragged about it. The whole thing, according to him, was over this girl he killed. He just wanted to get even with his boss and everybody else in his section. That's what it was all about – this girl." He shook his head, "Unbelievable. But to answer your question, General Morozov, there is no way to know whether he was actually in contact with foreign intelligence or simply hallucinating. He regularly lapses into hysteria and must be restrained with a straight jacket. Mostly it's just gibberish and a lot of foaming at the mouth."

"Yes," said General Morozov, "unbelievable, but we can't ignore it. The French? *Bozhe moi!* We didn't even think they were running operations in Moscow." He waved his arm wearily toward the door, dismissing them. "That will be all, gentlemen."

He headed straight to his spacious office on the tower's 21st floor. Sighing heavily, he dropped the file folders he had carried from the conference room onto his desk and walked to the high window overlooking the wooded acres surrounding the Yasenevo complex. He stood for a few moments just staring out the window. In the distance he could see the series of *dachas*, rustic wooden houses, and large villas, each with its own generous plot of land, reserved for the use of the service's senior officers.

Mohammed Attar had suddenly dropped off the map, a prime Line 'X' source. He thought back through his years of service to that time another world and over a decade away when he had been assigned to Warsaw as General Pavlov's deputy. The Poles had always been hard people to work with, never really partners. In fact, they hated the Russians, and the feeling was mutual. Russians and Poles had been at odds for centuries. Just look at how quickly the Poles had turned on them – *Solidarity* indeed!

Morozov had recognized the potential of Mohammed Attar as soon as he read the Polish police report and it had not been difficult at all to convince General Pavlov – the General always enjoyed poking the Poles in the ribs. Pavlov had been absolutely jovial following that meeting with the hapless Pozoga. It wasn't that he was especially enthusiastic about Attar as a potential agent; it was simply that Pozoga's discomfiture had put Pavlov in a good mood. He left the details to Morozov.

The trembling Lebanese was given a stark choice: cooperate with the KGB or be returned to the custody of the Poles and certain imprisonment for murder. If he agreed to cooperate, he would be permitted to leave Poland, but if he later failed to keep his promise, there was no place on earth where the long arm of KGB retribution could not reach. Mohammed was still very young – he had believed every word.

Morozov received considerable praise for the recruitment and had followed Attar's progress over the intervening years, if even from a distance as he moved up the ranks. The Russians were interested in OPEC oil pricing, and he had been surprised and delighted when the Prince hired the young Lebanese. Reams of information had been forthcoming, providing intimate personal details of members of the Saudi Royal Family, their inner politics and divided loyalties, their weaknesses. Russian petroleum policy also had benefited from knowing Saudi intentions in advance. And in London Attar had continued to demonstrate his value.

Morozov retained a sentimental attachment to the case, a predilection common among good case officers. He disliked the idea of it coming to an end under such ignominious circumstances.

Was this insane man even telling the truth? Had he betrayed Attar and other even more valuable sources?

Morozov's task was further complicated by the fact that the Lebanese agent's importance had been magnified recently because his work with the British Minister of State for Defense Procurement, James

Abbott, had been close to the formal recruitment stage. Chairman of the KGB Viktor Chebrikov, as well as First Chief Directorate head Vladimir Kryuchkov had been briefed on the juicy possibility.

Morozov had seen the press account of Abbot's accidental death, but now he wondered if it had really been an accident.

The highest authorities in the land would have to be warned of the catastrophic peril facing Directorate 'T' and the entire VPK acquisitions program. Morozov knew full well the extent of damage this could do to Soviet industry.

If this came about, Morozov suspected more than the French were behind it. The Russians could only wait and see what happened next.

Chapter 32

One morning about two months after Attar's disappearance, I walked into the front office with a large *café au lait* from the cafeteria in one hand and a sheaf of cables in the other.

"Terry's been here for a couple of hours already," announced Eileen. "He was called in early to read an eyes only cable from Headquarters. He said you should go right in."

Behind his big desk, Stoddard was still wearing his running suit. He habitually jogged every morning. "Sit down, Harry. There's some news from Langley."

I got a funny feeling that it concerned Barskikov. "Good news or bad news?" I asked.

"Depends on how you look at it." He slid the eyes only cable across the desk toward me. "We're debriefing a new KGB defector in Washington, and he mentioned Barsikov. He's apparently dead; shot as a spy."

I pushed some air through my lips. "Can that be confirmed?"

"After some digging, the open source folks dredged up a tiny death notice that appeared several weeks ago in *Pravda*."

"The poor bastard told me he didn't have long. I wonder how he was caught."

I thought back to that meeting in Kolomenskiy Park that seemed so long ago but in reality had been only a few months earlier. I had been puzzled at the time by his words: "I have nothing left to look forward to, and I wish for nothing more than to do as much damage as possible." His final words to me had been,

"You won't see me again."

"The defector's story is nearly unbelievable. It's about half-way down the first page there."

I read through the cable in my hands and laid it back on Stoddard's desk when I was finished. "He murdered a woman and nearly killed his boss?"

"And right at Yasenevo, to boot, if the defector is to be believed."

"We have to tell the French."

"Of course, Headquarters is preparing a formal report today. You'll deliver it to Picard as soon as it's in our hands."

"This changes a lot of things, you know."

"Of course. It throws open the doors now that there is no source protection issue. We're free to use all of Barsikov's information any way we like and as aggressively as we like. It's going to take the wind out of their sails.

The Soviet Union was going down.

Chapter 33

The French can be delightfully, wickedly vengeful. It can be fun if you're working with them rather than the object of their petulance. With a fresh load of DST-supplied ammunition, *Le Figaro* continued its venomous campaign against the Brits involved in *Al Sakir*. Picard was delighted when that bastion of British left-wing thought, *The Guardian*, joined the campaign. The Prime Minister found herself on the wrong end of fox and hounds. But wily as ever she eluded her pursuers and portrayed them as unpatriotic prigs. She didn't feel compelled to say anything about the French.

One of the reasons was that we provided the Brits with a copy of the Directorate T shopping list for the UK, as well as the identities of Brits who were witting or unwitting KGB collaborators.

When Barsikov effectively took himself out of the equation, he freed us up to use his information as flagrantly as we pleased. All over Europe governments were drawing up lists of KGB operatives to be declared *persona non grata*. Even the Swiss were getting into the act.

I huddled with Picard and Dominique Thibault in the down-at-heels DST conference room. Thibault was somewhat embarrassed by his first name, a perfectly fine name meaning something like "of the Lord," a description that might be considered at odds with the job of a counter-intelligence officer. But the real reason was that these days it's a name more often given to girls than boys. So Thibault preferred to be called "Dom."

We're all entitled to our little vanities.

"Well, what do you think?" Picard waved a hand over the document on the table between us.

Truth be told, I was impressed and amazed. The French and the Russians have played footsie for centuries, since Catherine the Great. For a very long time, the Russian court spoke only French, Russian being the language of the peasantry. Pushkin wrote poems, and Turgenev came to Paris to translate and popularize Russian literature. In sum, the French were convinced that they knew the Russians as well as anyone and knew how to handle relations with them better than the Americans. Barsikov may have convinced them otherwise. The document we were studying was a list of over one hundred Soviet officials the French Government intended to declare *persona non grata*. All of the names came from Barsikov's documents.

"That's pretty damned impressive, Jacques. Pretty damned impressive. It's a big step, and it makes a strong statement."

Picard smiled contentedly through the layer of blue smoke from Thibault's ever-present Gauloise.

There was one curiosity about the list of undesirable Soviets. Nikolay Kozlov, my weekly lunch partner, was not on it while nearly every one of his KGBnik colleagues, including the *Rezident*, was.

When he first arrived in Paris, the French requested traces on him, and we had been only too eager to identify him as KGB. I met Kozlov at the so-called "diplomatic club" on Avenue George V, just across the street from the swank Hotel George V. The club was a well-stocked pond for spies trolling for recruitment targets. Very few fish were actually hauled in, but it was good sport for all.

Kozlov and I had been flirting with one another for over a year, mostly on Uncle Sam's credit card. He was always willing to talk, if only obliquely when a sensitive topic was raised. I had yet to figure out if his willingness to meet so regularly with a well-known spook like me was evidence of what we called a "vulnerability" or if he had been tasked with keeping an eye on me. I wasn't on the circuit as much as when I had been young case officer on the make, and the Russians were probably curious about what I was up to in Paris.

It paid to be agnostic in cases like this, wait to see if a true vulnerability to recruitment bobbed to the surface, and be ready with a tailored pitch if it did. Kozlov and I weren't "friends;" we were more like jousting opponents who enjoyed a drink together at the end of a good match. Kozlov seemed to enjoy it as much as I.

But Kozlov should be on Picard's list, and he wasn't. What the hell did that mean? One possibility was that he was being targeted by the DST.

"It's a pretty comprehensive list, Jacques, but not every Russki spook is on it."

Picard glanced shiftily (I thought) at Thibault whose face remained expressionless. "We have our reasons," he said.

Bingo.

I couldn't be certain, of course. Kozlov wasn't the only name missing, but he was the only one I knew personally. This would bear watching. We might be reverting to the game of Ami versus frog. Who makes it to the Russian spy first? But even if they recruited him, what could the DST do with another agent in Moscow that they were incapable of running?

"When are you going to drop the hammer?" I asked.

"We'll send the list to the Foreign Ministry tomorrow."

I returned to the office in a state of gleeful anticipation of the imminent disaster for the KGB and speculating on how it would affect Kozlov. Our next lunch was scheduled for the following week. I wondered if he would show up.

Chapter 34

Kozlov showed up.

I was already seated at our usual table at the *Petit Colombier,* facing the entrance, of course, so I saw him come in. Good. For the price of lunch I would get an up-close and personal KGB reaction to the hasty and ignominious departure of literally hundreds of his fellow commies from various European capitals the week before. This would make Headquarters happy, almost justify the cost of a one-star meal, and leave me with a happy place in my mid-section.

The Russian shook hands solemnly. As soon as he was seated, out came the pack of Marlboros, and he stoked a coffin nail with a plastic lighter. He took a long draw and exhaled with a whoosh of breath. I couldn't tell whether it was a benign whoosh or a challenge. Regardless, it was all smoke.

He had to know I would be curious about what was going on in that huge mausoleum he and his comrades occupied in the Sixteenth Arrondisement. I wondered if he would be working from a script or give me an honest assessment ... as honest as a Soviet official could afford to be, that is.

"Hullo, Nikolay," I said, "How's it going?"

He took a long drag and locked eyes with me. "*Pozdravleniya,* Harry." He was congratulating me in Russian. There was irony in the phrase, but heretofore he'd insisted we speak English. The native language of *Perfide Albion* is widely spoken in France, but not so with Russian. I guessed he wanted to keep this conversation private. Or maybe he thought it would give him a linguistic advantage.

I answered in his language. "Congratulations? What for? I've done nothing."

"Maybe, maybe not."

"You're not referring to the sudden repatriation of your comrades to Mother Russia, are you?"

He continued to stare at me through the smoke, so I plowed on. "At least you're still here holding the fort. They'll make you a hero."

"Maybe I would have preferred to be sent home." He spoke quietly with a shake of his head.

There were different ways to respond to this. I didn't think flippancy would win me any points, so I decided to be sympathetic and just a tad provocative. "I think I can understand that."

This evoked a bitter smile. "Is that so?"

It was a cardinal rule that we never referred directly to one another's affiliation with mutually hostile intelligence services. Once that Rubicon was crossed, all bets were off. But we were cutting pretty close to the bone here.

"I mean, do you feel left out? Is it an insult that you were permitted to stay? Or have you figured out why, yet?"

His eyebrows met in a frown, and I saw his jaw tighten. Was it something I said? Maybe. Maybe not. Probably. He showed up for our regular lunch. Maybe he had something to get off his chest. I hoped I wasn't pushing too hard.

The waiter chose that moment to offer me a wine list and suggest that *le tourin d'ail doux* was a special of the chef today. Kozlov buried his face in the menu while I ordered a bottle of *Montrachet Bâtard*, assuming we might have fish to follow the soup. Something mild and buttery seemed to be in order for Kozlov's delicate temperament. I ordered seared white sturgeon with caviar *beurre blanc* for both of us.

Kozlov wasn't very talkative over the meal. I enjoyed the garlic soup, but he might as well have been spooning gruel into his mouth. Another restaurant I liked was *Le Copenhague* on the *Champs Elysees*. Not only was the Scandinavian cuisine excellent, but they provided an iced bottle of aquavit or vodka at the table. The Russian might have appreciated something heartier than white wine today.

The fish arrived, and Kozlov was still moody. Why was he here today if he didn't want to talk?

"Nikolay," I said, "I'll have to pay for this meal myself if you don't say something."

That evoked an upward twitch at the corners of his mouth. "I like smoked fish, Harry," he said, "not this tasteless white stuff."

I thought the sturgeon was really quite good.

"Well, hell, you should have spoken up when I ordered instead of sitting there with a look of doom on your face. Eat your potatoes. Russians like potatoes."

"If they're in liquid form," he said.

I placed knife and fork on my plate with a regretful glance at the remaining sturgeon and wine. "OK," I said, "Let's get out of here and go somewhere we can find liquid potatoes."

The waiter assumed a stricken expression at the sight of our unfinished meal but was assuaged by a generous tip. The French are stingy with their tips. Therefore, despite what people say, French waiters love

Americans ... unless they order steak well-done.

There was a bar on the corner of *Acacias* and *Avenue Carnot*, where we found a quiet table. I ordered a full bottle of *Stolichnaya* on ice and some smoked salmon. Ten minutes later Kozlov was in a more talkative mood.

"I have a problem, Harry."

No kidding. "Do you want to tell me about it?"

"It's my wife."

"Your wife?" I was taken totally off guard.

"I think she's being unfaithful to me."

Now, this was not what I was expecting. I thought he was glum about the mass expulsion of Russian spies. I knew his wife only slightly. But if there's anything that can take your mind off problems at work, it's an unfaithful wife.

There was occasionally some fooling around within the Russian colony, so this was not particularly earthshattering news. But it was a very personal subject that a Russian was unlikely to discuss with an American.

"I'm sorry to hear that, Nikolay. Are you sure?"

By now we were each on our third shot of vodka.

"No, but she's acting strange."

"Whom do you suspect? Is it one of the guys who were sent home?"

He tossed back another shot of vodka and reached for the bottle. "I think it's a Frenchman."

"How is that even possible?"

"We're not all locked up in cells after dark, you know. We do get out now and then."

"OK."

"In Moscow we had a nice apartment, thanks to

Svetlana's father. We had a two room place of our own on *Kutuzovskiy Prospekt*. Svetlana was accustomed to high standards at home. Where do you think we live here in Paris, in the greatest city in the world? We arrived full of excitement and expectation."

I knew that most of the Soviets assigned to Paris lived in a building not far from the embassy compound on *Boulevard Suchet*. I let him talk.

"Our building is in the 16th Arrondisement, the richest area of Paris. But we live in a communal apartment with three other families! We even have to share the kitchen and the toilets. In other words, we live worse in Paris than we did in Moscow. Svetlana is very unhappy. She told me last night that she wished we had been declared *persona non grata* along with the rest of them."

"So she wants to return to Moscow?" This was inconsistent with an affair with a Frenchman.

"She wishes we'd never left. And last night she said she might have another way out and threatened to leave me."

On top of being left out of the herd of spooks sent packing, if his wife ran away with a Frenchman, poor Nikolay would be in really big trouble.

"When it's appropriate, Svetlana and I attend receptions and dinners together – the happy Soviet couple."

He downed another shot. The bottle of *Stoli* was almost half-empty by now, and my eyes were beginning to cross. If this progressed through a second bottle I would have to pour myself into a taxi and go straight home where Kate would have to lay me out on the bed.

"There is a Frenchman who says he works in the

foreign ministry press office. We met him at a small dinner party about six months ago, and he offered to help me with some useful contacts. We've met several times since then, and he always insisted I bring Svetlana along. He showed us a lot of kindnesses, paying for everything, inviting us to nice restaurants."

"Do you think he's French intel?"

His head jerked up. "The French don't run intelligence operations against us."

If Barsikov had talked under interrogation, the Soviets should know already that he was working for the French. And even if he hadn't, the DST was broadcasting it among the European services. The press would run with it soon.

"What makes you think they're having an affair?"

"Svetlana has gone out alone several times over the past month. She's only supposed to go out with the other women, but she ignores the rule. When I ask, she gives a vague excuse."

"That's doesn't sound good, but are you sure it's this French guy and not one of your Russian comrades?"

"I would know if it was a Russian. No secrets are safe when you live in a communal apartment."

I could see his point. More importantly, his options were limited and unpleasant. His people would wonder why he was not on the expulsion list, and suspicion always wins out where Russians are concerned. If his wife ran away with a foreigner, it would be at the very least the end of his career. If he asked to be sent home, people would wonder why. His goose was already in the oven crisping to a golden brown.

"What can I do, Nikolay?"

"Can you check out this Frenchman?"

The poor sap harbored the forlorn hope that he could emerge without too deep a scratch, but I would play along.

"Sure. What's his name?"

"He says his name is Remy Blanchard."

"What happens if I check him out? What good would it do you?"

"At least I would know what I'm dealing with."

He suspected his wife had fallen into a honey trap.

After my recent collaboration with the French against the Russians, I was now being asked for help by a KGBnik. I was fast becoming a charity for needy espionage organizations.

"Can you let me have a picture of your wife?"

"Why?"

"It might come in handy." I'd met his wife once or twice, but I needed the photo.

He pulled out his wallet and extracted a snapshot of an attractive blond woman. "Take it."

"I think I should go now." I wanted to get out of there before he asked for a second bottle of vodka. "Can you make it to our usual lunch next week?"

"OK."

I left him there in the bar. I don't know if he ordered a second bottle.

Chapter 35

Success in espionage, as in many other undertakings, more often than not is determined by one's ability to take advantage of opportunities that are impossible to predict. Kozlov's predicament was one of these occasions.

Damn, but I loved this job.

Kozlov was probably correct in assuming that he was dealing with a honey trap. The question was who set the trap. Given the nationality of "Blanchard," the most likely candidate was the DGSE, followed by the DST.

I wondered if either of the French services was aware of my longstanding acquaintanceship with Kozlov. The DST was a highly capable internal security service. As with any such service, they controlled their turf and could mount sophisticated surveillance operations. The safest conclusion was that they knew I'd been meeting Kozlov for the past year.

Terry Stoddard and I discussed possibilities for the rest of the afternoon. I managed this despite the combined effects of Montrachet and Vodka, which is not a combination I recommend.

Stoddard said, "We could sit back and watch the soap opera play out to the end and maybe try to snatch Kozlov on the rebound."

This would be a passive/aggressive approach.

"We could mount our own surveillance operation against Svetlana Kozlova to find out what's really going on."

Stoddard was listing the possibilities so we could

knock down the least advisable ones, so I said, "Surveilling someone we think is targeted by the French risks running into their surveillance teams, and we'd end up butting heads and getting embarrassed."

He nodded, "Or we could come clean to the French that we know what they're up to and want to be cut in on their operation."

I said, "The best course would be to go to the French, specifically Picard and the DST." Stoddard was a very smart guy, and I trusted his judgment.

Insofar as we could trust a French service, we tended to trust the DST over the DGSE.

I got back to the apartment around six P.M. Despite the dinner Kate had prepared, my stomach rebelled at being asked to digest anything on top of the wine and vodka. Kate was displeased, so I told her about Kozlov and his wife.

"The poor woman," she said. "Your buddy, Kozlov, must be a real louse."

"I don't know. He seems like a nice enough guy to me."

She maneuvered her features into that expression women have when they come upon yet another confirmation that they are superior to men. "I'll bet he works all the time, comes home tired, and sometimes disappears for days at a time but can't tell her where he's going. She's left all alone to worry and fret until he gets back from whatever spook mission he's been given."

It took a few seconds, but even my addled brain picked up on this. "But I do exactly the same thing."

"Yes, you do, but you're not a louse. See the

difference?"

I grabbed her and gave her a big kiss on the lips. "Can you please put me to bed now?"

"OK, but I'm going to eat the dinner I spent an hour preparing and have some nice wine, too. So don't expect me to jump in there with you."

"I have nothing more in mind than sleeping it off, so you're safe."

There was a mischievous glint in her eyes. "So, alcohol makes me less desirable? Isn't it supposed to be the other way around?"

I couldn't win. "Kate," I said, "you are highly desirable at all times, but right now, I'm totally useless.

Chapter 36

The next morning the distinctive aroma of a Gauloise in the corridor at the *Place des Saussaies* forewarned me that Thibault was waiting with Picard. You could smoke in the finest restaurants in Paris in the eighties, although you risked really pissing off people who'd paid a couple of hundred dollars for a small plate of exquisitely prepared food and another bundle for a bottle of wine. Fortunately, the precincts of the DST offered no such luxuries, and I lit a short Montecristo No. 5 in self-defense.

"It's my turn to ask for some help." Given the way I'd "helped" the DST, I was opening with a weak hand hoping to draw into a straight.

Picard and Thibault raised their eyebrows in identical expressions of polite Gallic curiosity.

"What can we do for you, Harry?" asked Picard.

"I want to talk about Nikolay Kozlov, the *Novosti* correspondent."

Their expressions transitioned from curiosity to carefully controlled neutrality before Picard said, "What about him?"

"To start, you know he's a KGB thug, but he wasn't expelled with the rest of them."

Picard mustered up a tone of mild annoyance. "You're here to complain that he wasn't expelled?"

"Not at all. As a matter of fact, I'm glad he's still here. I've been developing him for nearly a year."

Thibault's mouth twitched upward at the corners, but he quickly resumed his bland expression, deferring to his boss to speak. But that little twitch said a lot.

Picard pursed his lips the way the French do when they want you to know they are thinking. He said, "Yes, we know."

"Were you watching him or me?"

"That's immaterial. We know."

Picard could be such a smug shit.

"What do you know about his wife?"

"His wife? Why do you ask?"

He sounded more worried than curious. Maybe that last card would yield a straight, after all.

"Someone, probably you guys, has set a honey trap for her.'"

Thibault actually blushed. Well, well, well.

Picard's voice was neutral. "How do you know this?"

Not "what makes you think this," but "how do you know this."

"Kozlov told me all about it yesterday. Who is Remy Blanchard?"

Thibault was pink from neck to brow by now, and I made a leap of faith. "Dom, you son of a gun, you've been romancing a Russian, haven't you."

Thibault opened his mouth, but Picard cut him off. "Why are you so interested, Harry. Were you about to pitch Kozlov?"

My cigar had gone out, and I took a moment to re-light it while I thought about how to proceed.

"I don't think he's ready. Recruiting Soviets is a lot like coaxing a timid animal out of the woods. You have to lay a trail of bait until he's eating out of your hand. Russians are not a trusting sort."

Picard pursed his lips again. "What do you know

about his wife?"

"She's attractive and unhappy. Kozlov probably hasn't paid enough attention to her, and that makes her easy prey."

"Would you excuse us for a moment?"

They stepped out of the room and closed the door.

Had the Barsikov operation convinced them they could poach on DGSE territory with utter disregard? They weren't equipped and did not have the skill to handle a defector, and the wife of a Russian, even the wife of a Russian spook, was not a particularly valuable asset. Maybe they were after Kozlov himself.

After a quarter of an hour they returned.

Picard said, "As you apparently have surmised, we have been working on Svetlana Kozlova. What you do not know is that she is a code clerk for the KGB *rezidentura*."

This was news to me.

"Are you sure?" I had to ask.

Thibault finally spoke. "That's what she says."

"I don't see how it's possible that she's able to get out on her own."

"It's her father," said Thibault. "He's real *nomenklatura*, and she can flaunt the rules."

"If that's true, she would be a major catch. What are the chances she'll defect?"

"We're working on it," said Picard. "There is still some distance to go. Her motivations are personal rather than ideological."

"Kozlov told me she was a spoiled *nomenklatura* brat who resented how they're forced to live here. She thinks she deserves better in a town like Paris. Even a privileged life in Moscow can't compete with what she sees all around her here. So what will you do with her if she comes over?"

"Exploit the information, of course."

"A code clerk would have unique access, but she can only carry so much information in her head. You'll want her to bring out crypto materials and files, if she can."

"Of course."

Crypto materials are pure gold. The Soviets would change their codes if they were compromised, but even the old materials would permit decryption of past intercepted traffic. I figured if the French were telling me this much, they wanted something.

"What do you want from us?" I asked.

Picard had the decency to be slightly embarrassed. "Maybe you could help with resettlement?"

Aha. Resettlement is an expensive process that eats up time as well as money. It's like adopting an ill-mannered child for which you will be eternally responsible.

The DST wanted the goodies, but hoped we would pay the bill.

"In exchange you would share any crypto she manages to get out?"

"Of course."

I told them I would think about it and headed back to the embassy.

I was certain of only one thing: it was highly unlikely that Svetlana Kozlova was a Soviet code clerk.

Chapter 37

In the first place, it was barely conceivable that a Russian code clerk could ever escape onto the streets unaccompanied. The rule with the Soviets was that code clerks were never permitted to venture away from official quarters alone. The risk was too great. So it required a real stretch of imagination to believe that one might actually be sleeping with a French counter-intel guy.

The first major Soviet defector after World War II was Igor Guzenko, a code clerk who defected from the Soviet Embassy in Ottawa in 1945. His revelations of pervasive Soviet intelligence operations in North America helped spark the Cold War.

"Maybe the Soviets are setting up the DST," I said to Terry Stoddard.

He groaned. "But I don't see the benefit to them. Temporary embarrassment of the DST seems hardly worth the effort. Are you certain she's not a code clerk?"

"It's not very likely. Svetlana is just out of the Embassy too much. There's also the fact that she and Nikolay live in a building separate from the Embassy. Code clerks usually live in the chancery. I just don't see the pampered daughter of a *nomenklatura* bigwig spending her days breaking out code. And I've never heard of a female KGB code clerk."

"Mmm. Why don't the French see this, I wonder."

"Maybe it's wishful thinking. They're still on a high after Barsikov."

"Should we share our suspicions with them?"

"It depends. If his wife actually defects Kozlov is

a dead duck. He thinks she's falling into a trap, but he's told no one but yours truly. That tells me he's angling for something besides confirmation that Svetlana is two-timing him with an enemy agent. He might be looking for a way out if the shit hits the fan."

"OK." Stoddard had reached a decision. "As good allies, we'll share our doubts about Svetlana with Picard and decline direct participation. They may decide to continue despite their limited means for resettlement. If they haven't already done so, they may turn to the DGSE for help."

The French had their own signals intelligence capabilities, housed with the DGSE, and they had been stealing secrets out of the air, including a lot of American secrets since 1946. In fact, they were probably stealing U.S. industrial and technological secrets faster than the KGB.

"And what do we do in that case?"

Stoddard smiled. "We sit back and watch while you maintain contact with Kozlov."

"And we pick him up on the rebound and leave the French to look after a useless defector."

"That's the idea."

Chapter 38

"I'm sorry to hear that." Jacques Picard was genuinely regretful when he heard our suspicions regarding Svetlana Kozlova. But this soon turned to suspicion.

I knew this because his next words were, "You're not trying to screw us, are you?"

"Of course not, Jacques. I'm just giving you our take on Svetlana. We have no indications she's a code clerk, and a lot of indications she's not. We have no interest in her."

"I think you're trying to screw us."

Frogs will be frogs. If they're not screwing you, they're certain you're screwing them. They may not be able to figure exactly how it's being done. They probably develop psychosomatic pains in the ass.

"I don't see how you can say that, Jacques. We're sharing our doubts so you can save a lot of time, trouble, and money. Besides, I don't think we're clever enough to mess around with you on your own turf."

"It would not be wise to try."

That didn't sound promising because I actually was planning to screw them. Better stated, I was planning to let them screw themselves.

"So they're unhappy with us?" asked Terry Stoddard.

It was nearing noon by the time I returned to the office, so we'd nipped over the Île de la Cité in the COS's chauffeured BMW for an Alsatian lunch at a favorite spot.

"They're looking for a coup, and they're afraid

we'll snatch it away from them." I lifted my mug of Kronenbourg. "Here's to Froggo-Yankee cooperation."

Stoddard had been a French scholar for practically his entire life. He shot a reproachful look in my direction. "The problem is we don't know what Kozlov is really up to asking you for help, and we can't be sure his wife will defect. He could denounce her and maybe escape with his skin."

"You still think the Soviets are playing a game to even the score?"

"I don't see where they'd go with that. I've never heard of a double honey trap. But they like dangles, and they're bellowing about the expulsions being nothing more than a provocation."

"Only time will tell."

"What will you tell Kozlov?"

"Thibault is using a backstopped identity with Svetlana, one Kozlov can't penetrate. So I'll give him the cover story."

"The DST won't like that."

"I know," I said, "It'll be ticklish."

"Yes, but one way or the other, we're already into it."

The *choucroute* and sausage began to feel heavy in my stomach.

*****

The following day I went home for lunch to find Kate fuming. I mentally checked but couldn't think of anything I had done to cause it.

"I paid a visit to the *fromagerie* on *Place de la Madeleine* this morning," she said. "Someone was following me."

Kate had proven deft at spotting surveillance when we were in Eastern Europe. I'd learned to trust her instincts.

"I thought we were finished with this kind of thing, but here it is again, and in Paris of all places. Do you think it's the Russians?"

"No such luck. More likely it's the French."

"Because of this Kozlov thing?"

"Probably."

"How long will this go on?"

"Until this Kozlov thing is resolved, I suppose."

"I don't like it."

"Me neither."

"You should lodge a complaint."

"It wouldn't do any good. They think I'm up to something. I half expected to have a tail, but not on you."

"How should we handle it?"

"Don't react. Just pretend you don't notice."

Kate was in no danger, but I was worried about the meeting scheduled with Kozlov. It wouldn't do for the French to see anything out of the ordinary. The lunch meeting was coming up fast, and I had to move our contacts to another level invisible to the DST.

Chapter 39

When I entered the restaurant I saw two guys in cheap suits at a table with an excellent view of mine pretending to read the menu. Picard wasn't taking any chances. I half expected that my table was bugged, as well. The DST were putting on a full-court press, and they didn't mind being obvious about it.

Kozlov was nervous when he sat down. I didn't doubt that he had spotted our watchers, as well. I knew he was eager to hear what I'd learned in the intervening week since our vodka-soaked conversation, but he wisely said nothing about it, and neither did I.

It would do no good to complain to Picard because he would simply deny that he had set the dogs loose. Fortunately, I was prepared.

When Kozlov pulled out his Marlboros, I shoved a matchbook across the tabletop to him before he could pull out his plastic lighter. He gave me a quizzical look and opened it. Inside I had written the address of a safehouse and a date and time.

Kozlov was good. He didn't bat an eye as he ripped out a match and lit his cigarette. He slipped the matchbook into his pocket without a further glance, and we discussed world affairs for the rest of the meal.

I noticed that the DST watchdogs ordered the cheapest items on the menu and a pitcher of house wine.

This was a big step. If Kozlov accepted a clandestine meeting with a CIA officer, we were well on our way to recruitment. Given the circumstances, I doubted he would remain in place, but he possessed information of undoubted value to our counterintelligence folks.

I'd set the meeting for mid-morning the following Sunday. First thing Saturday, Kate and I headed for our favorite inn in Compiegne. The idea was that, if the DST followed us, I would slip out in the wee hours of Sunday morning to meet a Station officer who would drive me back to Paris and get me back later to rejoin my wife. I was sure that Kozlov would take similar precautions to evade surveillance.

I didn't like the looks of a man and woman seated across the dining room from us that evening. They were more interested in us than the food, which wasn't bad. Not enough to be certain, but enough to make me cautious.

I slipped out of our room at four AM and made it to the waiting car with no sign that I had been seen. Kate would stay in the room until I returned, and our car in the parking lot should reassure the surveillants that we were still there.

The safehouse was in the 17th Arrondisement, near the *Parc Monceau.* The officer who had driven me took up position in the park where he could observe the entrance to the building. He would warn me if he spotted anything untoward. It was a simple plan, but effective.

Kozlov was ten minutes late, and I had begun to think he wouldn't show up. He looked nervous when I let him through the door.

I'd bought some croissants and had a pot of coffee ready, but he wasn't hungry. He knew the stakes as well as I.

"How much time do you have, Nikolay?"

"Not more than an hour before someone gets curious," he said.

"OK, first things first. I'd like to meet you here again in a week, same time but with an alternate two days later. OK?"

He knew the drill as well as I and lit a cigarette with slightly trembling hands before answering. "OK, but only if you have the information I requested."

"Have some coffee." I filled our cups. I needed the caffeine. "I checked out the man you described and can tell you that he is with the press office, and he is romancing your wife. He could be working with French intelligence, or the affair could be genuine."

If Picard discovered I had said even this much, my ass would be on a plane to Washington before I could say *sacre bleu*. It all depended on whether Kozlov and the KGB were playing a game as Terry Stoddard suspected.

Kozlov's shoulders sagged under the weight of this news. "You're sure?"

"As sure as I can be. Sorry, Nikolay."

"It will be the end of me," he said.

"Maybe, maybe not. Depends on what you do."

He knew exactly what I meant, but he just stared at me. He was trying to figure out if he could trust me.

"I need to know more," he said.

"Why don't you confront your wife?"

"I don't know what she would say."

"Only one way to find out."

"Then what?"

The idea was to be sympathetic, to be his friend,

to gain his complete trust. We'd known one another for over a year, and now I'd laid my cards on the table face up. He might risk coming over to us, but if he didn't the seed was planted, and we might get a crack at him another time even if his wife didn't leave him. You just never know, and you have to be patient.

"Do you think French intelligence is trying to recruit my wife?"

"Maybe."

"But what would they do with her? She has no official function and knows nothing of my work."

"Maybe they're really after you."

"Then they have a strange way of going about it."

"Maybe they think you'll defect to them, too."

"To the French? After this? They think they'll force me into a corner?"

He was indignant now.

"Could be. You're stationed here. You know things that would interest them."

I was taking a chance because he might start thinking he could come to terms with them or even that I was working him in tandem with the French. I didn't want to put any ideas in his head, but sometimes the truth can work wonders.

He crushed his cigarette in the ashtray with unneeded force. "Never. These bastards are destroying my life."

So far, so good.

"Well, be that as it may, you know you have other friends, other places you could go if it becomes necessary."

"I never thought I would have a conversation like

this."

"I know, but we've known one another for a long time, and I can help if you like. So what are you going to do now?"

"Maybe I should talk to Svetlana as you suggest. We might be able to work things out. She should think about how her actions will affect her father back in Moscow. She's a very selfish person."

"Good," I said but didn't mean it. "Let's meet here again in a week and you can let me know how it turns out. I don't think we should have lunch on Thursday."

"Yes. I noticed the watchers, too."

As an added precaution, I gave him a phone number and protocol for emergency contact in case something should break before our next meeting.

Two hours later the car dropped me off some distance from the hotel, and I lit a cigar and walked back through the woods. There was a lot to think about, and it was anybody's guess how things would turn out. Nikolay might somehow get his wayward wife back to Moscow, and we would never hear of him again. I was certain of only one thing: you can't play poker unless you ante up.

Chapter 40

Kozlov had a rough week. I knew this because he activated the emergency contact protocol the Wednesday after our meeting. This could have meant anything, but it's human nature to anticipate the worst, in this case the worst for Kozlov - his wife had defected.

We'd heard nothing more from the DST about their honey trap, and I was dragging an unwonted pair of watchers everywhere I went. It was almost always the same two guys from the restaurant, and French discretion was not in their repertoire. They just looked bored but determined in their cheap suits. I almost felt sorry for them.

Not really.

I stepped out of the Embassy for a stroll along the *Faubourg St. Honoré,* and they were still there. I don't like small, cramped spaces, but a short time later I was in the trunk of an Embassy car rolling out of the motor pool garage. I was released from this confinement somewhere in the *Bois de Boulogne,* an area where unusual sightings are commonplace, especially after dark.

I grabbed a taxi to the *Park Monceau* and slipped into the safehouse to wait for Kozlov. He arrived shortly after noon looking like he hadn't slept much the night before.

"Are you clean?" I asked.

"I've been running all night." He was disheveled and nearly gasping. "My wife didn't come home yesterday evening, and I suspected the worst. I got out of the apartment around one AM, but they followed my car. I finally lost them near *Montparnasse*, ditched the car, and just walked the streets until now."

"Will you be missed at work today?"

"Maybe not for a while yet. Nobody saw when I left the apartment."

"Tell me what happened."

"I did as you suggested and just asked her flat out if she was having an affair."

I waited.

"It was hard to find the right moment. We live in a communal apartment, you know. So I took her for a walk along the river. She denied everything, but I think she was scared."

"What do you want to do now?" This was a pretty important question. He was teetering on the brink, and it was my job to push him over.

"You don't think I'll go back, do you."

"Hey, Nikolay, that's entirely up to you. But I can help if you want me to."

"Defect?"

"If that's what you want. I can't make that decision for you."

Nikolay was not a happy camper, and I knew he wouldn't blame me or the CIA for his predicament. I wanted him to see us as a friendly port in a storm.

"I've got to think about all this, try to figure something out."

"You can stay here as long as you like. The fridge and pantry are stocked. It should be safe for you to stay here at least until tonight. You could return to the Embassy with no one the wiser. I'll be back in a few hours."

I was taking a chance leaving him alone, but

there was really nothing more I could do or say. He had a big decision to make.

I walked a block to *Boulevard Malsherbes* and caught a cab that dropped me on the Rue de Rivoli a short walk from the Embassy. When I entered the front office, Eileen informed me that Jaques Picard wanted to see me. I turned on my heel and made the familiar trek to Place des Saussaies. The two bad suits were still behind me.

Picard didn't bother with formalities. "We have a problem," he said.

"Oh?"

"We have Kozlov's wife."

"Already?"

"Her husband forced her into it."

"How did he do that?"

"He started asking questions, and she got scared. She called Thibault yesterday, *et voila.*"

"So what's the problem?"

"She wants to go back."

"Already?" This was an unexpected twist that could put a kink in my plans for Kozlov, as well. "What happened?"

"I think she figured out she'd been tricked."

"You mean Thibault didn't sweep her into his arms and propose marriage?"

"Thibault is already married."

"That didn't stop him from bedding her."

Picard squinted and pursed his lips. *"C'est la vie."*

"So what are you going to do?"

He had the grace to look embarrassed. "Will you

take her?"

I really love the French. They'd screwed up royally and had a useless defector on their hands, a defector who wanted to re-defect, and they hoped Uncle Sam would bail them out.

"She's not a code clerk, is she?"

"Apparently you were right about that. She made it up to make the affair spicier."

I was trying to figure out if taking the woman off Picard's hands was a good idea or a bad one. It didn't take long to decide. "What in the world would we do with an unwilling and useless Russian?"

"It would mean a great deal to us." Those words cost Picard a lot.

"Why do you think she would want to go to the CIA? You said she wants to go home."

"You could offer her a lot of money."

Why does everyone assume the CIA has money to burn?

"I don't think that'll fly, Jacques. There's such a thing as going to the well too often."

I thought there was a way to use this.

"It's definitely a no-go," I continued. "You'll just have to let her go. You can't very well hold her against her will. Maybe she can slip back without anyone noticing she's been gone. How long have you had her?"

"Since yesterday afternoon. And the Russians know. They've inquired at the Foreign Ministry to report her missing. Her husband has disappeared, as well."

Picard must have known that I'd slipped surveillance that morning. They couldn't have missed my return to the embassy. He cocked a suspicious eyebrow. "Do you know anything about that?"

I conjured up what I hoped was an air of innocence. "First I've heard of it, Jacques. I would have thought you guys would be after him, too, maybe try to use his wife to blackmail him into defecting along with her."

"We know you've been in contact with him."

"We already talked about that. I've had lunch with him a few times. He's a hard case. Maybe he's just out looking for his wife."

I left a very unhappy Jacques Picard and beat feet back to the embassy to bring Terry Stoddard up to speed.

"What do you think they'll do?" he asked.

"They'll have to let her go. Not even the DST would hold her against her will."

"And Kozlov?"

"I think we can use this, but it'll be tricky. I'm heading back to the safehouse now."

Stoddard grinned his agreement. "Be careful. They're probably still watching you."

Two hours later I arrived at the safehouse hoping Kozlov was still there. A cloud of acrid smoke hit me in the face when I opened the door, which meant he was.

Kozlov was standing at the window looking like he was considering jumping out. He scanned me with worried eyes.

"I have news, Nikolay. But this is only between

you and me - even if you return to the Embassy."

"Tell me," he said.

"The French do have your wife."

His face sagged even more.

"But we may be able to get her back."

Hope hiked his face up a notch, but then he turned suspicious. "What do you mean? Are you in this with the French?"

"Hell, Nikolay, if I was telling the French how to do this thing, it would be working a lot better."

"What do you have in mind?"

"Well, I found out that Svetlana was really disappointed when she found out her boyfriend had duped her, and now she wants to go back home. There's no way the French can hold her against her will."

Kozlov only looked confused, so I continued. "So, if we can get you back to your embassy before she turns up, we might be able to salvage something."

"You'd help me go back?"

"If that's what you want to do. The other option is always open."

"Why would you do this?"

"Someday you may decide we can work together. Things are changing in Moscow, and you may need a friend like me."

"What if the French won't let Svetlana go?"

"You can probably think something up that would force their hand. She could have been kidnapped, for instance."

Now this was really playing dirty with the French, but they'd screwed things up so badly they had it coming.

"What will I say when I get back to the Embassy?"

The fact that he was asking me for advice was a positive sign.

"Tell them you've been searching for your wife. They've already reported her missing, by the way, and they're wondering where you are, too."

Kozlov might not be able to pull it off, but he was a smart guy, and the story was plausible.

"You know they'll send us home right away."

"I know. I'm going to give you a signal site in Moscow. After a while, maybe six months or a year, and you're sure you're not under any suspicion, you can mark it. I'm giving you a dead drop site, too, and a week after you leave the signal, we'll load it with further instructions."

I held my breath. Well, I held my breath figuratively. In fact, I lit a cigar and watched for his reaction as I held out the written instructions I'd prepared before leaving the station.

He accepted the instructions. Big step.

"You'll have to memorize them before you leave here," I said. "No way you should carry them around."

His hand was trembling again, and he looked from the paper to me. "I guess it can do no harm. I've come this far," he said. "But understand I'm not promising anything."

"OK. Like I've been telling you, it's up to you. No pressure."

He committed the instructions to memory. He paused at the door before leaving and said, "Harry, I have one gift for you. They know it was you."

"Who knows I was what?"

"They know it was you in Moscow with Barsikov."

"Why would they think a thing like that?"

"Despite what some may think, we do have technology in the Soviet Union. Barsikov described you when he was interrogated, and they captured some good images from airport cameras. It wasn't difficult to match them to old photos of you. We have quite a lot of them, you know."

"Maybe they're right and maybe they're wrong, Nikolay. What difference does it make?"

He gave me a long stare. "It means that you should be very careful." With that he disappeared out the door.

I finished my cigar and tidied things up, before catching a cab back to the Embassy. I didn't bother with being dropped off a distance away. I'd done what I could, and whatever happened now, it would be months before we knew Kozlov's final decision. As for his warning, I'd been careful for years, whenever possible, of course.

In view of what happened in the following few years, maybe I should have paid more heed, but no one can read the future with 100% clarity.

Chapter 41

Things got interesting the two days later when a Soviet Embassy press release accused the French government of attempting to kidnap the wife of Nikolay Kozlov, Novosti correspondent in Paris. They claimed she had been snatched off the street and taken to an undisclosed location where French intelligence agents falsely accused her of shoplifting and pressured her to lure her husband into a trap. This bizarre action, declared the Soviets, was a further escalation of the provocations represented by the recent mass expulsion of innocent Soviet diplomats. A formal complaint was conveyed through diplomatic channels to the French Foreign Ministry.

No one believed it, of course, but it put the DST under a cloud. Picard remained suspicious, but he couldn't figure out what had happened. The Soviets bundled Kozlov and his wife onto the first flight to Moscow. That meant no more contact with him and left the French scratching their heads.

They stopped following me, and for that I was grateful.

There was no way of knowing how Kozlov fared with his superiors. He and Svetlana appeared on Moscow television to confirm the kidnap story and add further embellishments. They answered some cooked questions from tame reporters. Svetlana managed to look authentically indignant. I hoped her influential father could pull enough strings to keep her out of the gulag. I hoped even more that Kozlov was still in the

KGB.

Maybe he'd managed to pull off the deception with his superiors and keep his job; maybe he hadn't. There was a reasonable chance we would hear from him. Whether his purpose would be to begin cooperation with us or to ambush some poor case officer in Moscow was unknown. Patience and taking risks are virtues for intelligence officers.

As often as not it's the poor sods who agree to cooperate with foreign intelligence services who pay the price in the end.

Chapter 42

Chop-Chop

There are no appeals in Riyadh, where justice is swift and administered with the sharp edge of the executioner's sword.

Mohammed Attar sought no appeal. He just wished they would get on with it. His body ached from the *mahabith* beatings, but he knew there would be no more pain in Paradise. He ached more for death, for an end to the sorry confusion his life had been – a twisted path from callow youth to cynical adulthood. Thank God he had met the Sheik who had put meaning back into his existence.

His "trial" had been a matter of a few minutes in a closed room with three Imams. Saudi justice strongly preferred confession over evidence, and confessions did not necessarily have to be voluntary. But Mohammed had been only too happy to comply, roundly condemning the Saudi regime for the money-grubbing, debauched apostates that they were. His vehemence had shocked the judges who had quickly concluded the "trial" with a verdict of guilty and a sentence of death.

In an act of routine cruelty, they did not inform him of the date set for his execution, and he waited in his cell, hoping every morning that this would be the day. If the time passed nine A.M., he knew he would have to wait a day longer. All executions in Riyadh took place in "Chop Chop Square" at precisely nine A.M. They were no longer announced publicly, so that if you were having your morning tea at a café on the small, nondescript square you could well become witness to a beheading.

After morning prayers on the fifth day following his trial they came for him at last. Two uniformed guards entered his cell and instructed him to put on a long white garment, a sort of *dishdasha*, and then cuffed his hands behind his back. He was led into the courtyard where a yellow van was waiting to transport them. When the van finally drew to a stop and the doors opened, he recognized the place. Curiosity had drawn him there in his youth. It was just a small, drab square surrounded by shops, with a large metal grate at its center. There were not many people there, and it seemed almost a casual affair to chop off someone's head. It occurred to Mohammed that the quotidian setting served to emphasize how acceptable and commonplace such a death was in The Kingdom.

The two guards helped him step out of the van, one on each side holding his arm. They were surprised that he did not resist, did not collapse in fear, but rather walked steadily between them the few steps to the spot of execution.

Ignoring the guards and the small crowd that

had gathered, Mohammed concentrated his attention on the executioner, a hulking black man at least six and a half feet tall dressed in a long white *dishdasha* and checkered *iqal.* He stood waiting with feet planted apart, hands resting on the hilt of a long, curved sword.

The guards pushed Mohammed to a kneeling position in front of the executioner. He did not resist. The executioner asked if he would like to recite the *Shahada,* the declaration of faith that sets Muslims apart from the rest of the world, and Mohammed was grateful for the opportunity. "*Ash-hadu an laa ilaaha illallah.* I bear witness that there is no god but Allah. *Wa ash-hadu anna Muhammadan rasullah.* And I bear witness that Muhammad is the messenger of Allah."

As soon as he was finished someone jabbed his side with a stick, and Mohammed's body went taught as he stretched his neck and the razor sharp blade flashed downward in a swift arc.

Before the darkness claimed him Mohammed's last thought was that he would have some interesting questions for God.

The End

The Author

Michael R. Davidson was raised in the Mid-West. Heeding President Kennedy's call for more young Americans to learn Russian he studied the language, and military service took him to the White House where he served as translator for the Moscow-Washington "Hotline." His language abilities attracted the attention of the Central Intelligence Agency, and following his military service Mr. Davidson spent the next 28 years as a Clandestine Services officer. Seventeen of those years were spent abroad in a variety of sensitive posts working against the Soviet Union and the Warsaw Pact. In the private sector he worked as a business owner and security and economic development consultant before devoting full time to his writing.

Also by Michael R. Davidson

Did the Cold War end or did the KGB find a way to retain its power and dominate the new Russian Federation? "Harry's Rules" is an espionage thriller set against the backdrop of post-Soviet Russia in the early 1990's.

Who killed President John F. Kennedy? A long buried secret that could change the course of history draws murder to a quiet Washington suburb. Only an exiled CIA officer can solve a mystery that both the White House and the Kremlin will protect at all costs.

Find them at: www.michaelrdavidson.com
All books also available via Amazon.com

The Dove

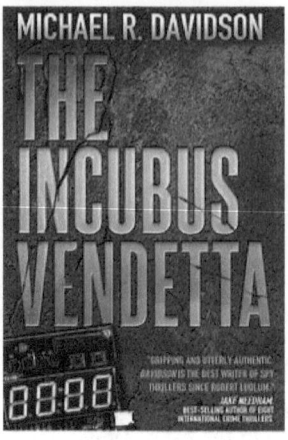

Deposed Russian president Shurgin is desperate to punish those who brought about his downfall, and nothing will get in his way. A suicide bomber and a serial killer are his chosen instruments. A quiet afternoon in Brussels is shattered by unspeakable horror, and a madman leaves a trail of blood in Washington. But his targets are anything but helpless, and Harry Connolly vows to put an end to Shurgin once and for all.

The Russians set a trap, and Harry Connolly's aka Ewan Ramsay's beloved Sasha falls into it. Captured by the sadistic and cruel Russian mafioso Zhenya Lomonosov and his henchman, Sasha will soon be secretly transported to Moscow into the hands of Vitaliy Mikhailovich Shurgin. The Mossad and Ewan Ramsay are faced with the necessity to mount a bold rescue operation against Zhenya's nearly impregnable stronghold.

Find them at: www.michaelrdavidson.com
All books also available via Amazon.com

Disillusioned by Spain's failing fortunes in the 30-Years-War, Eduardo Macías leaves the Army of Flanders and sets out for home. Eduardo's reputation as a valorous soldier leads to his being named Captain of the Santa Hermandad, a Spanish force charged with protecting the people and maintaining the law. He is forced to accept a mission by officials of the Holy Inquisition to investigate an alleged case of heresy involving a nobleman with ancient royal ties. What Eduardo discovers places him in a dangerous situation at odds with the Inquisition, and he must choose between upholding his honor. and excommunication.

In 1492 victorious King Fernando of Aragon forces the daughter of the last Muslim ruler in Andalusia to become his concubine as a gesture of "reconciliation." The product of their coupling, a secret Muslim with an abiding hatred for his father, founds a line that nurtures the flame of vengeance through the centuries. Now, with the assistance of Iranian Intelligence his descendant threatens a nuclear holocaust if the ancient lands of Andalusia are not returned to him. Facing insurmountable odds resourceful Spanish cop Alberto Macías and CIA officer Robert Strachey must risk their lives and careers in a desperate race against time.

Find them at: www.michaelrdavidson.com

The Dove

All books also available via Amazon.com

A controversial Miami judge is murdered in a Washington hotel room. Homicide detective Krystal Murphy identifies an ideal suspect, a person with motive and opportunity. Following the suspect's trail to Miami, she is confronted by an unspeakable tragedy. Convinced her initial instincts were wrong, she teams with a Miami detective. When more people associated with the case begin turning up dead, Krystal finds herself in a race against time before she herself becomes the next victim of an increasingly

Find it at: www.michaelrdavidson.com
All books also available via Amazon.com

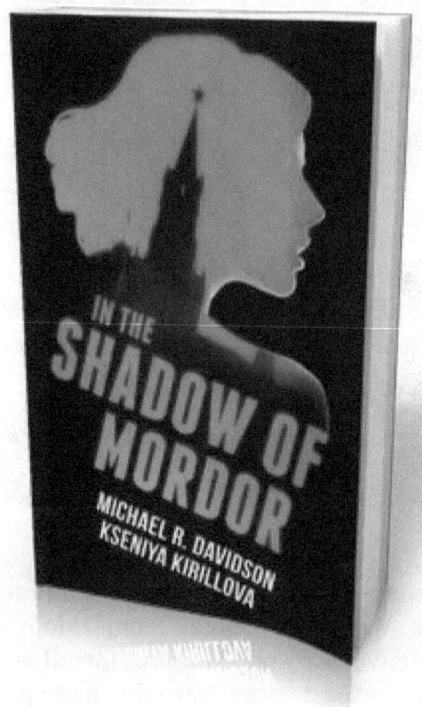

Michael R. Davidson teams with Russian author Kseniya Kirillova to pen a tale torn from the realities of today's Russia.

Michael R. Davidson and Kseniya Kirillova team up for the second time in the exciting sequel to IN THE SHADOW OF MORDOR.

Find it at: www.michaelrdavidson.com
All books also available via Amazon.com

www.ingramcontent.com/pod-product-compliance
Lightning Source LLC
Chambersburg PA
CBHW021030130626
46552CB00005B/1774